I0622060

DEPRIVATION

Jana Nolan

DEPRIVATION

Jana Nolan

Earth Star Publications
Eckert, Colorado

FIRST EDITION
First Printing August 2018

All Rights Reserved
Copyright © 2018 Jana Nolan

This book may not be reproduced in whole, or in part by photocopy, mechanical, or any other means without the express written consent of the author. For information, contact Earth Star Publications. For publisher's current address information, go to www.earthstarpublications.com

ISBN 978-0-944851-54-8

Printed in the United States of America

DEDICATION

This book is dedicated to my six grown sons:

Terry Frasier
Tracy Frasier
Don Frasier
Jonathan Nolan
Jesse Nolan
Darren Nolan

The day each one of you were born my life changed. Every day has been a blessing from God, who made me your mother. My love to all of you forever.

CONTENTS

PART I
STORM BEFORE THE CALM

PART II
FEAR AND WHAT IT BRINGS

PART III
ON THE ROAD AGAIN

PART IV
THE TOWN THAT DIDN'T EXIST

PART V
THE FACE BEHIND THE MASK

INTRODUCTION

For those of you that aren't familiar with any of my books, or my style of writing, I would like to say that this one took me on a journey in my mind to bring you stories that will thrill and chill you.

I grew up in a small town called Montrose, Colorado. Most of my stories have revolved around a small town atmosphere, but with this book, I am taking you in a different direction.

With all of my stories, I like to give my readers a look at the unknown, and leave you wondering if any of them could actually happen in our time period of life.

Sit back and enjoy the stories that will give you a ride of a lifetime. When you have finished reading them, remember that they are only fiction, or are they?

The first story, "STORM BEFORE THE CALM," is about a man who grew up in a dysfunctional family searching for answers to why his life has been turned upside down.

The second story, "FEAR AND WHAT IT BRINGS," is about a woman who learns how to live a normal life with help from many people. She grows up with a whole new perspective of where she needs to be in her mind to make this happen.

The third story, "ON THE ROAD AGAIN," is about a young woman who chooses a career that takes her to a place in search of a family member who wouldn't have survived without her help.

The fourth story, "THE TOWN THAT DIDN'T EXIST," is about a man who grew to realize that the journey he was living was different than anything that he ever could have imagined it to be.

The fifth story, "THE FACE BEHIND THE MASK," is about two women who travel to a place to get away from everyday reality, where one of the women finds her worst nightmare.

I named the book DEPRIVATION because of the stories themselves. Not just in my book, but in everyone's life, we find that we have been deprived of something that we feel we deserved to have.

As with all of my books, I try to give my readers a lesson of what can maybe happen to them or an idea of what someone else in their life has experienced.

Now that I have shared with you a brief summary of what each story is about, it is up to you, the reader, to decide if any of these tales are capable of happening at any given moment, or if they are just something that an author, such as myself, completely made up to captivate her readers. Fact or fiction?

However you interpret the book, remember that there are strange happenings every day that surround us, or out of bad choices we find ourselves in the middle of. With all of this in mind, enjoy the fictional stories that will make you think.

Jana Nolan

PART I

STORM BEFORE THE CALM

—1—

THE UNEXPECTED

Today is a warm, clear sky day in the Woodberry Cemetery as I stand here amongst many people, listening to a minister talking about redemption and how my half-sister would always be loved and remembered by her family and friends.

Standing next to me is her mother, my father, and her boyfriend. People have come together in this spot to say goodbye to a young woman that I barely knew.

She had been my half-sister for twenty-one years, and I am ashamed to say that I really didn't take the time to get to know her. Several years ago, when my parents decided to divorce, I was only four years old. I didn't understand why my father didn't come home at night as he had always done before.

As I grew older, Mother explained to me that Father didn't live with us any longer, and was living in a different town for now. None of this made sense to me at the time, but because she had told me this, I believed what she said and accepted Father visiting us whenever he could.

Each year that went by became easier for me, as I not only looked forward to his visits, but also was involved with my friends and school.

Mother never talked about Father when he wasn't there, and for years I had no idea what his life consisted of, or even where he was living.

In fact, I was 10 years old when I was told by him that he had a daughter by another woman that he lived with for a while. He said at that time he was not allowed to visit her, and that someday he would bring her with him so that I could see my half-sister. Each year I waited to meet her, and finally I gave up and realized that it probably wasn't going to happen.

Three years ago, when I was getting ready to leave the office for the day, my receptionist came in and told me that there was a young woman waiting to see me before I left.

I told her to show her in and that after I did leave the office, to only direct important calls to my home phone.

She agreed and told the young woman that she could come in now. When she entered the room, she smiled at me. I looked at her and was fairly sure that she wasn't one of my business acquaintances as she was attractive but young, and wearing simple clothes like someone who didn't have a lot of money.

I told her to have a seat, and if she would like a glass of water, I would be happy to get it for her. She said no.

"My name is Trinity Austin. This might come as a surprise to you, but I am your half-sister," she said.

"No. Many years ago, my father told me that he had a child by another woman, but failed to tell me your name," I replied.

"It took me quite a while to find you. I never really got to know my father, other than a few brief visits, which only lasted a couple of hours at a time. My mother refused to let him be a part of my life, but during a visit he did tell me your name. Now that I am a grown woman, I wanted to find you," she said.

"I, too, waited years to meet you after Father told me about you, and finally I gave up. It is nice to finally meet you, Trinity," I commented.

"I have tried to find our father as well, and I keep getting told that he is living out of the country and that no one is sure when or if he will return. Do you have an address for him, or a phone number where he can be reached?" she asked.

"No, I don't. After I reached a certain age, Father became very distant to me as well. I heard that he was living in Kentucky for a while. After that, I haven't heard any other news about him. I can tell you that with the job that he has had for many years, it can take him anywhere in the world," I said.

"Thank you for letting me know this. Mother refuses to tell me anything. I am hoping that at least you and I can get to know each other," she responded.

"Yes, Trinity, we can. I, too, have questions that maybe you can answer. Would you like to go out for a cup of coffee? I would invite you to dinner if tonight I wasn't expecting so many phone calls at my home later. Would another day work for you for dinner, either at my home or in a restaurant?" I asked.

"That would be very nice. I will try to answer as many of your questions that I can answer correctly," she spoke.

Before we left the office, I informed my receptionist that anyone could reach me at home later this evening.

We left to go to a small café for coffee that was close by. We sat there and talked for a couple of hours and then she said that she would come by another time to see me, so that we could try to make up for lost time.

I only had one other phone call from her, telling me that she was still trying to find Father, and when she could, she would let me know exactly where he was. This was two years ago. I didn't see her alive again.

My name is Travis Roberts. I am a broker for a large company in Westport, Michigan. As you can see, I come from a dysfunctional family.

After the minister was completely done speaking, I watched as my father walked away without a word to Trinity's mother. Of course she was crying, but my father didn't shed a tear. To me, this was disrespectful in its own way, and I confronted him about it.

"Father, what is wrong with you?" I asked.

"What do you mean, Travis?" he said.

"This is your daughter and you didn't cry at her funeral! This is really not right," I replied.

"Travis, I may have fathered her, but I wasn't allowed to see her except for a few times. I am sorry for her death, but I never was able to know her. If this seems strange to you, then I am sorry for that," Father commented as he walked away.

Feeling like I owed my half-sister something, I went to her mother and apologized for my father's actions and gave her a heartfelt hug. I didn't know this woman, but that was the least I could do. Trinity had a short life and I was wishing that somehow I could have gotten to know her better.

Then I, too, turned around and walked away.

As I was driving back to Westport, I couldn't help but wonder what my father had done to cause a woman so much pain that she forbade him from seeing his own daughter. I knew that I was very young when Mother and Father had divorced. Not once did I ask either one of them why they did this. No matter what the reason was, now being a grown man, I wasn't sure if it even mattered to me anymore. All I knew was that, like Trinity, I was deprived of my father most of the time.

I had one more day of work and then my friend Nick and I were going to the lake to go fishing for three or four days. His wife was going to visit her aunt, and so he asked me if he could join me.

When I walked into my office, I sat down at my desk to finish what work I needed to get done before leaving. I had emails waiting for me to respond to. In my inbox was a strange email that should have been spam. When I read it, I was convinced that it came from someone that either didn't want to be known by me, or a message that was meant to go to someone else. It didn't have a subject to it. All it said was,

"We didn't have much time together. I will be coming back to get you."

I replied back with a short message, asking who I was communicating with, and the message was returned, saying that there was no such email address listed. This kind of gave me the creeps. For whatever reason why this happened, I wasn't into playing games back and forth. If this was meant as a joke, it was a sick one. I didn't think it was very funny.

I finished my day and soon I was leaving to go home to pack. Nick would be meeting me at the lake, where I had a lake home. Hopefully, it would be a restful time for both of us.

—2—

QUESTIONS AND MORE

The next morning, I was up early and ready for a fun time catching trout, and maybe hiking as well. Everything was loaded in the car and I was ready to walk out the door. The phone rang and it was Nick calling.

"Hello," I said.

I just wanted to let you know that I am on my way to the lake. Marcy already left. Can't wait to catch some fish," Nick replied.

"Me too. I will see you in a few hours," I said.

I was out the door and on my way to my car when I had a weird feeling that someone was watching me. This was something I hadn't experienced. Even with neighbors watching me, I didn't feel this way. Maybe I was still feeling creepy after being in a cemetery yesterday. Funerals always have that effect on me.

I continued to walk to my car, and after I got in, I looked at my rear-view mirror and saw a woman's necklace hanging from it. This had not been there before. All of these strange things coming at me within a couple of days made me wonder who was trying to contact me, and why were they going about it this way?

Within a few hours, I was driving up to my lake home. Nick was there already, waiting on me. After I got out of my car, I grabbed my fishing pole and tackle box.

"Hey, buddy, are you ready to catch some big fish?" Nick asked.

"I have been ready all week. Let's go in the house and put our things away," I replied.

After I unlocked the door, we were on our way in. The next process was taking the sheets off the furniture. Before we went to the lake, we had a light lunch and did some talking.

"Thank you again for letting me join you for this adventure. With Marcy gone for a week, that old house would have gotten pretty lonely," he said.

"No problem, my friend. Actually, I am happy that you wanted to join me. Since yesterday I have had some pretty weird things happening to me, and even though I am a man and shouldn't let things bother me, I have to tell you that whatever or whoever this is who is doing these things to scare me could be working," I told him.

"Why would anyone want to do this to you?" he asked.

"I am not sure. Yesterday I went to my half-sister's funeral. She was way too young to have been killed like she was. I only met her one time for a brief visit. I was around 10 years old when my father told me that he had a daughter by another woman. He said that someday he would bring her to meet me, but for years, growing up, I waited and it didn't happen.

"I had put her out of my mind when, one day at my office, she showed up to meet me. Her name was Trinity. She was very young and said that she had been told about me as well. She said that it took her a while to locate me. She asked where our father was living as she wanted to see him as well, and that no one knew where he was at.

"I told her that he traveled around the world with the job that he had, and the last time I knew where he was at was when he lived in Kentucky. I asked her to join me for some coffee and we could talk as I, too, had some questions for her as well. She told me that her mother refused his visits and wouldn't tell her anything. My own mother never talked about Father, but when I did ask a question, she would answer it the best that she could. This makes me wonder what exactly Father did to her mother, who denied him to see his own child like that.

"We talked about this over coffee, and Trinity said that she didn't know the answer to that question as her mother wouldn't tell her. We talked about many things for a couple of hours, and then she told me that she would keep in touch so that we could go out to dinner like I had promised her to do soon.

"I only heard from her one other time. She told me that when she found out where our father was, she would let me know. I didn't hear from her again, and then a couple of years later, I got a call from her boyfriend, telling me that she had been stabbed to death as she slept. He said that he was the one who had found her. He then told me her funeral was yesterday and where it was at.

"It bothered me to see her lying in the casket like that. She had a very short life, and apparently there was more to her than I knew about, as why else would anyone want to kill her? I even checked my phone, to see if I had a missed call from her, asking me for help. There was none.

"Yesterday at the cemetery, Father didn't cry, and after the minister was finished, just before they lowered her casket into the ground, he started walking away. The entire time he didn't speak to the mother of his child and it upset me. I kept wondering how he could be so cold-hearted, so I confronted him about it. He just told me that he couldn't cry because he had been denied so much time of seeing her that he really didn't know her.

"The sad part is that he could have found her when she was grown up and tried to be a part of her life, and he didn't do this. I felt like even though none of this was my fault, I owed her mother something, so I gave her a hug and told her that I was very sorry for her loss. Then I left.

"When I got back to Westport, I went to my office to take care of the emails and to finish up for this trip. In my inbox was one email without a subject, and all it said was, 'We didn't have much time together. I will be coming back to get you.' I tried to respond back, wanting to know who it was that sent it, but got my email back, stating that the email address didn't exist. This creeped me out, but the more I thought about it, the more I considered it to be a sick joke. So I left work to go home

"Today, when I got in my car, I found a necklace with a locket that a woman would wear hanging on my rear-view mirror. I tried opening it, to see what pictures were inside, and it was stuck. So I decided that none of these weird things are going to ruin my trip here, and I will try to get the locket open when I return to Westport. This is strange, and once again, Nick, I am happy that you are here."

"I have heard some crazy occurrences before in my life, but I think this one tops them all," he said. "If I had a half-sister and this happened to me, Travis, I would be wondering why my own father reacted the way that he did. I know that people handle grief in different ways, but with you telling me what he said and how he behaved, it sounds to me like he didn't care at all, unless his bitterness toward her mother was getting in the way of his true feelings.

"As for the email, that is weird. Normally, I would think that it was sent to the wrong person and maybe the service provider caught this after you read it and just returned the one that you got back to whoever sent it, but with it not having an existing email address after you replied back is creepy all right.

"As for the necklace with the locket, maybe it belongs to your mother with a picture of you and her inside of it, and she just put it on your mirror, knowing that you would find it as she was late for work. That might have been her way of giving you something that was important to her. For now, I wouldn't read too much into that," he commented.

"You are probably right. For now I think I am done telling you about either ghost stories or a creepy incident that took place. Let's get ready and go to the lake," I said.

"That would probably be for the best, as I don't like cemeteries either, and after a point we will be going to bed to sleep with one eye open all night." He laughed.

When we were ready to leave, I locked the door and we walked in the direction of the lake. There was still plenty of daylight left and we had our hearts set on a fish fry for supper. After a couple of hours with no luck fishing, the thunder and lightning moved in and the sky opened up and rain started pouring down on us. It was as if Mother Nature had her own plans for us. We grabbed our poles and started running toward the house. It was a good idea that we had brought food to eat, as the fish remained in the lake for the day.

When we returned to the house, we sat around and talked about our fun times from high school, and all of the camping trips we had taken. One of the stories that we talked about was our trip with two other kids that we were friends with, going to the hills to camp with one of the other two boys' young brother tagging along with us. That night after the young boy went to sleep, we all stood outside the tent and roared like a bear. It frightened the kid, and when our friend returned home and his little brother told their mom and dad about it, our friend wasn't able to hang out with us for a while.

We had relived our youth and were ready to go to bed, being hopeful that the next day brought sunshine,

The next morning, the rain had stopped, and at 4 a.m. we were out of bed and sitting in my kitchen, drinking coffee. As I prepared a breakfast of scrambled eggs, ham and hash browns for Nick and myself, we talked again.

"That was quite the storm last night, Travis! I thought that tree next to your house was going to break off and come flying through a window," Nick said.

"I tried to go to sleep, but every time the lightning flashed, I was watching the window. I thought I saw a person outside with a black cape looking through the window a couple of times. This person was standing at my window with hands on the glass. I am sure my imagination was all that it was, but it did keep me awake until I finally was so tired, I went to sleep," I replied.

"This morning, before we go to the lake, we can check the ground for footprints. If there was anyone there, it would show in the mud," he said.

"That would be a good idea. As far as I know, I haven't done anything to make someone so mad that now they are out to hurt me, but I guess with me being a broker, you never know," I said, laughing.

"If they are out to get you, then they probably are out to get me as well, as you and I work for the same company. About twenty years ago, before you and I started to work there, one of the men that was a client ended up hanging himself. No one saw this coming. He was a nice man and liked to tell jokes to everyone, and all of the employees really liked him.

"When they questioned his wife about why her husband might do this, the only thing that she said was that because of all the responsibility he had, he became deeply depressed. He thought he saw someone following him one night after work, and when he went to report it to the sheriff, he was told there was nothing they could or would do, unless he gave them a good reason to check out his complaint. His wife said that after that happened, he was quieter than usual and didn't want to go to work, for fear of his life. Finally, I guess that the company told him that if he didn't go to work, he better look for a new job. His wife and himself had bought a huge home, nice cars, and a lot of other things that they could have done without, and so he knew that if he got fired, he would lose everything.

"So he went back to work. About a month later, they found his body dangling from a light fixture in the main bedroom, with a note that said that he was still afraid and wasn't going to wait for whomever it was to kill him, and that he was just going to do it himself. With what happened to him, it had everyone at work nervous because they believed that they would be next in line for the killer, or killers to go after.

"After a few years, the employees started to relax and realized that maybe the reason why this had happened didn't have anything to do with his job, and maybe his family life could have been the cause. Since then, nothing strange has occurred until a couple of days ago...with you," Nick responded.

"Wow! This is getting more weird every day. When we leave here, I am going to do some investigating of my own. I don't want the man dangling at the end of the light fixture to be me," I said.

By then, breakfast was ready and we had worked up quite the appetite, talking about doom and gloom. This had to stop as we went there to have fun.

In an hour we were on our way again to the lake, when we checked outside the window of my bedroom. There were no footprints in the dirt and mud, so again I must have been half awake and dreaming, thinking that this was happening.

Because of all the rain, the fish were hungry and Nick and I were pulling fish out, right and left. It didn't take us long to get our limit. We knew that we would be having a fish fry tonight for dinner. Once again, the clouds started rolling in and it wasn't long and the downpour of rain started again. We were on our way back to the house when I remembered that I had forgotten to grab my tackle box, and so I told Nick that I would be right behind him. I turned around and went back to the lake.

After I grabbed the tackle box and was walking on the trail leading to my front door, I was looking around, and in the trees I saw a person standing beside one, looking back at me. Whoever it was had on men's clothing, and the hair had been pulled back into a ponytail. This person, even with the rain, was wearing sunglasses. If it wasn't raining so hard, I would have walked over there to talk to the person, but the sky opened up more and the lightning was flashing all around me. I needed shelter and by the time I had returned home, I was soaked and cold.

Nick wanted to know what had taken me so long. I made up something as the ghost stories were going to ruin his trip and mine if I kept talking about strange things taking place, especially when I was the only one around to see or to feel it. I said that my shoe string kept coming untied and I had to keep stopping to fix it before proceeding onto the house.

That night we did have plenty of fish to eat. Nothing I had eaten since the last time that I was there had tasted as good as the trout out of that lake.

Once again we spent the evening talking and enjoying the great outdoors and the beauty that we had in between rain and storms, when we could look out the window at the trees, mountains and the wildlife that ran through the yard. All in all, we were having a good time, like the night before. About 11:00 p.m. we got tired and decided to go to bed. Another day of maybe fishing and hiking was planned for the next day.

In the morning, once again I fixed us some food to take with us and we talked. Today we were going to hike and then fish. There was a bunch of country that even I hadn't seen for a while, and so with sandwiches wrapped and in our coats, we were on our way out the front door. We decided to leave the fishing gear behind on the porch and come back for it later.

We started out walking around the lake. When we got to the spot where I had seen that person, I stopped. Lying on the ground in front of me was a pair of binoculars. At that moment, I felt as if someone was not just watching me, but Nick as well, and because of the heavy rain the day before, whoever it was decided to leave in a hurry. Maybe the binoculars fell out of a pocket, or had accidentally dropped. I picked them up and continued to walk faster to catch up with Nick.

When we reached the house, we got our fishing supplies and started walking to the lake. I had an eerie feeling the rest of the day and knew that when I did get back home, I had some people to see and some questions to ask.

It wasn't long and we were on our way back up the trail with, once again, no fish. So tonight for supper would be steak cooked on my grill inside, and whatever else I could find to go with it. As we ate, again we talked about days past in our lives. Not just in school, but since we had grown up. Nick shared memories with me as I did with him.

That night Nick called his wife and told her that we would be leaving tomorrow sometime, and that he would be home later in the day. He also said that we had fun and that he had gotten to eat an old-fashioned fish fry, and he was happy about that. With everything that was happening, I too was happy that he had come with me.

After seeing the binoculars on the ground and a person watching me, I knew that for some unknown reason someone was either trying to get to me, or to scare me. They were doing a good job of it.

—3—

FAST THINKING

The next morning, Nick and I woke up to another down-pour of rain. It looked like the clouds were there to stay for the entire time that we had planned to be there, so we decided to leave and come back another time, when the weather was better.

After coffee, we placed sheets on the furniture and grabbed what we had brought with us. Nick told me that in spite of the rain, he had a fun time and was looking forward to the next time that we came here. I told him that my door here would always be open for him and his wife, if they wanted to come here when I couldn't. We walked away and were on our way back to Westport.

Nick didn't waste any time on leaving, and was driving faster than I was. I wasn't in a big hurry to return home or to the office, so I drove slower. When I was on the highway, a car that didn't see me pulled out in front of me. I was going too fast to slow down enough to keep from hitting the other car, and decided to pass it instead. When I was about to, I noticed a large pickup coming toward me, and I knew that I was in trouble.

When I stepped on the brakes to slow down, I found out that I had no brakes. My car kept going at the same speed, and I was approaching the spot where I would be going down a hill. I kept pumping the brakes and trying to use my emergency brake to stop. That didn't work either. If I kept going, my car would be driving faster and I would be pushing the car in front of me down a long steep hill, or I would hit the back of it.

There was only one thing for me to do, in order to make sure that the other drivers were safe, and that was to turn my wheel to the right and pray that I survived the crash.

When I left the highway, my car was going sixty miles an hour. I found myself driving over rocks, tree limbs, and finally a quick stop just before I hit a tree. This was an experience that I never wanted to happen to me again.

The truck that was passing me when I caught up with the back of the car in front of me had a driver that paid attention and had seen me air-planning through the air off the highway, and he pulled over to stop. He came running over to me.

"Are you all right?" he asked.

"I think I am, but I am not sure that my car is," I replied.

"When I saw you struggling, I tried to put my brakes on so that you could pass before I reached you and the other car, but we were all going too fast, and it happened too quick. Are you sure you are all right?" the truck driver asked.

"I don't see any blood, so I think so," I replied.

"Try opening your door," he said.

I did open the door and stepped out of my car. I was okay, but very confused at how this could have happened as the brakes had worked fine when I drove to the lake.

"As you can see, I am fine. I will call a tow truck when I get to Westport. Is there a way that you can take me home?" I asked.

"Sure, I can do that. I have a stop to make down the road, but after that I will be going back there myself. You are welcome to tag along until I can get you where you want to go. Are you sure you don't need to see a doctor?" he asked.

"No, really, I am fine. I just want to go home," I said.

The truck driver took my word that what I'd said was true and soon we were in his truck, driving to the place that he was delivering firewood.

"What brings you out this far?" the driver asked.

"I have a home a ways down the highway. A friend and I just came from there after fishing for a while," I replied.

"What happened back there?" he asked.

"I saw the car in front of me pulling out onto the highway, and I was going to pass it, but then I noticed you and knew that I didn't have enough time, so I started applying the brakes. The only problem was that I had none. I even tried using the emergency brake and it failed as well. I had no choice but to leave the highway or cause a huge accident," I said.

"When was the last time you checked to see if you had brake fluid? Maybe you ran out."

"I had the car serviced the day before I went to the lake."

"I am not trying to scare you, but maybe someone cut your brake lines," he said.

"Trust me, I have already thought of that. After my car is towed to a shop, I will have them check for that," I replied.

For several days now, my life had been full of mysteries. In my mind I knew of no one who would want me killed. My nerves were wearing thin, and whoever was doing all of this to me knew it. It all started the day of the funeral in that cemetery, or was I just losing my mind, imagining the worst when this could have just been an accident? Maybe the place that changed the fluids failed to get the cap on tight, and for some reason it had drained out, or maybe gotten water in a line from all of the rain that we had there.

My not knowing much about the maintenance of a vehicle made it hard for me to figure out what really could have taken place. The email the other day could have been one that was misdirected to me instead of to the person that it was supposed to go to. The necklace, like Nick said, might have come from my mother. She might have been in a hurry to get to work and didn't have time to knock on my door to tell me about it. I had continually been letting my mind be obsessed with too many things. Maybe it was time to relax and wait for proof that someone had tampered with my car.

That night, when I did arrive home in Westport, I called my insurance company to report the accident. They informed me that they would call their towing company to give them the information on where they could retrieve my car. It would be tomorrow, and they assured me that they would do a thorough check to see what had caused my brakes to react the way they had. I was tired from all of the wonderment of what was happening to me, and went to bed.

While sleeping, because of my mind being unsettled, I had a dream that woke me up with a cold sweat. I dreamed I was walking on a trail in the woods near a lake with my friend Nick behind me. Ahead of us was a mountain that we would need to climb to get to a place we were going to. The more we walked, the closer we came to the mountain. But before we could get to it, the mountain started moving farther away from us again.

I was walking slower and my feet wouldn't move any faster. I was struggling to walk. When I turned around to talk to Nick, he was nowhere in sight. When I looked to my left, I saw him dangling from a tree with his head barely connected. I heard a woman laughing out loud. I couldn't run or walk as my feet were sinking into the ground I was standing on. I was yelling for someone to help me when I woke up.

Sitting up abruptly in bed, I rested my elbows on my knees with my head in my hands. I sat there awhile, thinking about what or if there was a message in the dream. To me, the mountains simulated a big obstacle that I could be facing right now. Nick, being my best friend, was with me at the lake for a fishing trip. This was why he was with me in my dream. Him dangling from a tree must have come from the story he told me about a man that was a client at our company who had hung himself from a light fixture, where as in my dream it was a tree.

I knew I had been in a hurry to get answers for many of the questions I had, and so this was probably why my feet wouldn't move faster, but became slower. The ground I was sinking into had to have been the ground from all the rain which caused it to turn to mud. Everything that had been bothering me for days finally found an escape through a dream. It was nearing the time when I was to wake up anyway, so I just got out of bed, not wanting to go back to sleep.

Later in the morning, after a car rental was delivered to me, I was on my way to work. I stopped at Mother's home briefly to talk to her, seeing her curtains pulled shut. Even though her car was parked in her driveway, she was not at home. This was nothing that hadn't happened before, so I left her a note, telling her to call me.

After I walked into my office, I called Nick to tell him what had happened to me after we parted our ways yesterday. He apologized for leaving me in the dust at the house, and I told him that neither one of us had any idea what was going to happen, and that the good part was that I was all right.

My car was anyone's guess as I had to wait on the insurance company to call me, to give me the good or bad news. He asked me if I wanted to come to the race track with him this weekend, and I told him that I would see as I might have some other things that might need to get done right away. I didn't go into detail telling him what they were.

My receptionist had left for the day and I hadn't even checked my desk to see what had piled up while I was gone. When I walked over to it, to sit down, I noticed something that again I didn't expect. A dead black rose had been placed in the center of my desk. Right away, I got on the phone to call Judy, my receptionist, to ask her why she had set it there.

"Hello," Judy said.

"Judy, what is with the dead rose?" I asked.

"Excuse me. I am not sure what you are talking about," Judy replied.

"When I went to sit down at my desk, I found a dead black rose in the middle of it. I assumed you had put it there for a reason," I said.

"Travis, why would I set a dead flower on your desk?" she commented, laughing.

"I wasn't sure why you would do that, Judy, unless it was some kind of a joke," I said.

"No. I wouldn't put anything like that on anyone's desk. A dead rose is a sign of death. Especially a black one, Travis. Are you all right?" she asked.

"I guess so. Thank you for telling me this, Judy. I will see you tomorrow," I said before hanging up the phone.

Now things were getting creepy again. Someone was trying to either drive me insane or make me think that I already was.

Once again it was a call to Nick.

"Hello," Nick answered.

"Nick, can I come downstairs and talk to you?" I asked.

"Yes, I'm not busy at the moment. Are you all right, Travis?" he asked.

"I am beginning to wonder. See you in about five minutes," I replied.

I practically ran down the stairs to Nick's office. When I opened the door, Nick told his receptionist that we would be talking for a while and not to disturb us. We went into his office and he shut the door.

"You look like you have seen a ghost, Travis. What is wrong with you?" he asked.

"After I spoke to you, I went to my desk to get started on papers that I thought had piled up while we were gone. Instead of finding papers, I found a single dead black rose sitting in the middle of my desk. Judy left for the day several hours before I got there, and so I immediately called her to ask her why she put it there. She didn't know anything about it, stating that it is a sign of death. I feel like someone or something is messing with me, Nick," I explained.

"Did you bring the rose with you in your pocket?" he asked.

"No, Nick. I just left it laying there on the desk. Who would be sick enough to do things like this to me?" I asked.

"I don't know of anyone that dislikes you, Travis. This has to be coming from someone outside the company and the building. Do you know of anyone who would do this to you, who might just be joking around and really not meaning you any harm?" he asked.

"No, I don't. I really don't have a lot of friends other than you and a few more guys that I have known for years. None of them would do this to me, and if they did, there would be a note attached, saying, 'Okay, we fooled you,' " I commented.

"Do you think the police should be told about all of this?" Nick asked.

"I'm still alive. There is nothing that they would do as they, too, would think all of this is just a sick joke by someone," I said.

"This is true. I'm afraid you are right. Would you like to come stay with us for a while, until all of these bizarre happenings stop?" he asked.

"Not now, Nick. Later, I might need to take you up on your offer, but it is time for me to start getting answers, and I have to work with facts and not assumptions," I responded.

Nick said that he understood, and I walked back up to my office. When I went again to my desk, the black rose had disappeared. It was as if it hadn't happened. Now things were becoming supernatural, and I was more freaked out than ever.

—4—

MORE DREAMS

The rest of the day I just sat in my chair, waiting for the ceiling to fall in on me, or the phone to ring, telling me that the psychiatric ward was coming to get me. I was fairly sure that I wasn't crazy, but all of this was starting to get to me.

I also was waiting for my mother to call me back. I wanted to ask her about the necklace that had the locket. She didn't call, so I went home.

When I walked through my front door, the phone was ringing. It was my insurance company calling me.

"Hello," I said.

"Is this Travis?" a woman said.

"Yes, it is. I recognize your phone number. What did you learn about my car?" I asked.

"Our towing company went to get it this morning. Your brake line had no indication of anything being wrong with it. There might have been air in your brakes. We will get it fixed and get back to you," she said.

"There is no way that the brakes could just have air in them as they worked fine when I drove my car to the lake. I think that you better check again a little closer," I replied.

"We can do this, but it is going to cost you some money as we will need to take it to a different place to get checked out," she said.

"I don't care about this! I want it done right, and you

people aren't doing this!" I commented.

"All right, I will have them take it someplace else. It will be a couple more days before we know anything," she responded.

"That's fine! I just want it done right!" I said firmly. I was so discouraged that I felt like my personality was changing. I knew that there was something wrong with my car, and it wasn't air in the brakes.

I went to the kitchen to fix myself a strong cup of coffee, and then I called my mother's home phone. Still no answer from her.

After eating, I went upstairs to take a bath. I thought that sitting in a tub would help me relax in order to get a good night of sleep. The phone rang again, so I sat down on my bed to answer it. It was Nick calling again.

"Hello, Nick," I said.

"How are things now, Travis?" he asked.

"Strange as usual. After I left you today and went back to my office to do some work at the desk, the black rose was gone. I know that I didn't imagine it being there, and I locked the door and left work. When I got home, my insurance company called me to tell me that they had been told my car had air in the brake lines, and that this is why I had no brakes. My car drove fine when I was going to the lake. I know I got a little too angry with the woman I was talking to. I told her to get it checked out better as they were wrong. She told me that it will get checked by a different place and that it will be a couple more days before they know anything different," I said.

"I'm sorry. I know that for about a week now you have been having nothing but bad news and things happening to you, Travis. I am getting worried about you and would really like it if you would take me up on my offer of you coming here to stay for a while," Nick responded.

"I know that you want me there and I appreciate it, but if someone is trying to get to me, there is no way that I am going to involve you two in this mess. I will be fine. I think I just need to have a good night of sleep. Surely this will end soon," I said.

"I hope so. If not, just come here to stay."

"I will," I told him.

Our conversation ended and by then I was too tired to even take a bath. I just wanted to go to sleep. I lay down on the bed without undressing and closed my eyes. Within a couple of minutes I was sound asleep.

Once again I had a nightmare. I was walking through the Woodberry Cemetery. It was dark with a full moon. I was stopping to look at names on the tombstones. In my dream I wasn't sure who I was looking for. I was just wandering around in a daze. I saw many people dressed in different clothes, stumbling as they passed me, saying things like, "What are you doing here, Travis? Why did you come back here? Join us, Travis. You know that you want to be with us."

The more I turned around, looking at a hundred people coming at me, and circling me to talk, the dizzier I became. Then, from out of the ground in front of a tombstone, I saw a black dead rose. Before I could reach for it, I saw a hand come from under the ground and it grabbed my ankle., It kept pulling on my foot and I couldn't move. All the people that surrounded me were laughing, and one of them said, "See, you know you belong with us here." At that time, being terrified, I again woke up in a cold sweat.

This time I didn't sit there, thinking about what the dream meant. It was too scary for me to even try to decipher what it was about. I got up out of bed and went back downstairs.

Finally, after several hours, I went to sleep in my chair until morning. This time when I woke up, I was certain that within a few days I would need to go back to the cemetery again. Maybe Trinity was trying to tell me something from her grave, and the only way she could do this was through my dreams.

For fear of Nick thinking I was going crazy, I chose not to mention anything else bad to him. The last thing I wanted or needed was for my best friend, or anyone else at work, wondering if I was off my rocker.

After I ate breakfast, I went to work as usual. Not knowing what to expect, I was ready for just about anything. Today Judy would be at her desk and maybe the unknown wouldn't happen to me. When I got into the elevator from the parking garage, I pushed the button for the first floor. From there I would take the stairs, like I always did.

About halfway into it, the elevator came to a stop. I waited for the door to open for someone else to get on it, but no one did, and the door wouldn't open. I picked up the red phone inside it to call for help and the phone was dead. I was stuck. I pushed the emergency button, and again it didn't work. It was as if someone knew my routine every day and was watching and waiting for me.

An hour or two passed as I sat and waited inside it, hoping that my air supply didn't run out or someone didn't do something like cut a cable so that the elevator would go crashing to the bottom. While I waited, I had many things I was thinking about. Finally, the door opened. No one was standing there, waiting to get on it. Again, this was too scary for words.

I walked into my office and the first thing that Judy said to me was, "Where have you been?"

"I was stuck on an elevator, Judy," I said, laughing.

"Did you ever find out who gave you the dead rose?" she asked.

"I am not sure, but thinking a girl by the name of Trinity did," I said as I walked away.

Judy said nothing, and I was ready to get started on my work. I hadn't done much for a while and knew that today I had to do as much as I could. I had to put my mind to rest for now.

Around 1:00 p.m. I received the call from my mother that I had been expecting. I could barely hear her, and only could get bits and pieces from her conversation to me. She said that she was traveling back from Florida and would see me in a couple of days. At least I knew she was all right.

After my day was done, I went home to see if there was a message on my phone from the insurance company. Again there was nothing. I would wait one more day before calling them back.

When it became time for me to go to sleep, I was fighting it. Being afraid of another nightmare, I wanted to avoid it by staying awake. I fought it for as long as I could, and then once again I was sitting in the living room chair, sleeping.

Around 2:00 a.m. I was awakened by a tapping sound coming from the outside of the window pane. I got up to look, but couldn't see anything. When I turned away for a minute to look for a flashlight, I heard the tapping sound again. When I turned around, I saw the image of a woman with both her arms up in the air, leaning against the glass. I could see the white dress she was wearing and the long blonde hair. Her eyes were staring at me with anger.

I ran to the front door on the assumption that the woman would still be staring through my window. I needed to see what she was doing there and why! By the time I got outside to my window, she was gone. She had disappeared into the night. Her hair looked like Trinity's. I knew that there was no way that Trinity could be staring at me through a window. She was resting in the Woodberry Cemetery, where she would be throughout eternity. Again, with questions on my mind that weren't getting answered, I was awake for the rest of the night.

When I went to work the next day, I needed peace of mind. There were too many questions that weren't getting answered, and in order for me to find the answers, I had to be able to take time off to go wherever I needed to go, no matter where it took me. I told Judy that I would be out of the office for a week or two and that there would be no way to reach me by telephone or email. I was going on a road trip.

I walked out of my office and back to the rental car. When I arrived home, I had phone calls to make, and once again a visit with my mother to ask about the necklace. Only she could explain that mystery, or should I say that I *hoped* she could. There was a message for me on my answering machine.

It came from my insurance company, saying that they had made a mistake and my brake lines *had* been tampered with. They went on to say that my car was trashed and that they would call me again with a settlement on it.

This explained what I already pretty much believed had happened. I wasn't going to wait around for a phone call from them, to know how much of a settlement I was going to get. So I walked back out of my home and went to where they had taken my car. I retrieved all my personal items from the car and called the insurance company back, telling them that I was not going to be available to talk to them for a couple of weeks.

My next stop was a dealership where I bought a new car. After that, I called the rental company to come and get the one I had been using, and went to my mother's home.

After I walked to her patio door, I knocked and she came to see who was visiting her.

"Did you have fun on your trip, Mother?" I asked.

"Yes. I rode the bus to your Aunt Mary's home. We had a great time. It was nice to see her again," she replied.

"I'm happy that you got away for a while. I know that was good for you. I have a question for you, and I am hoping that you can answer it. Days ago, when I was in my car leaving to go to the lake, I saw a necklace hanging from my rearview mirror. At the time I tried to open it and couldn't. I think that it was placed there by you before you left. It has a locket on it for pictures. Did you give me this?" I asked.

"No, I didn't. Can I see the locket?" she asked.

I took the necklace out of my pocket and showed it to her.

"I thought maybe it might have been one that belonged to your father's mother, but as I look closely at it, I can see that it isn't the same one," Mother said.

"If it wasn't you that did this, can you tell me whether Father would have done this?" I asked.

"I doubt it, son. He doesn't think about things like this. Have you tried opening it up since the other day?"

"No, but we can right now," I said.

I tried very hard to get the locket open and couldn't. It appeared to be glued shut for some reason. Mother suggested that I take it to a jewelry store to see if they could use something on it that would fix it, and I agreed that I would do this.

After telling her goodbye, I was out the door and on my way to drop the necklace off. I would have two answers before long. My brakes were tampered with and soon I'd know who the pictures were of inside the locket.

I dropped off the necklace and went back home. It was time to see if I could get an answer from my Aunt Mary on where my father was living. He was going to be the next person to speak with.

When I walked through my door, I had a message from the jeweler, telling me that it would be a couple of days before he could work on the locket. He said that it had been stuck together with glue that he was not familiar with, and he would figure it out.

I went into the kitchen to get some coffee and then I was calling my Aunt Mary.

"Hello," Aunt Mary answered.

"Hello, Aunt Mary. It is good to speak to you again," I said.

"Oh hello, Travis. How nice it is to speak to you as well. If you are calling to talk to your mother, she left a couple of days ago on the bus, to go back home," she replied.

"I already know that she made it home safely. Thank you. The reason why I am calling you is to see if you know where Father is living right now," I responded.

"Right now, Travis, he is living in a little town not far from Westport. At the moment, he is out of town on business, but he should be back there in a couple of days. The name of the town is Greenburo," she commented.

"I know right where that is. Before I go there, I will call

you again for an address. I want to surprise him, so please don't tell him that I am coming," I said.

"What a nice surprise! I won't say a word," she said.

I thanked her again and told her that I would be calling her back within a couple of days. By then, I would have the locket and could take it there myself, to see if he was the one who had hung it in my car, and explain to him everything that I was going through, in hopes that he might be able to answer maybe one question that I had.

I had called Nick and told him that I was on vacation for a couple of weeks and that I would give him a call when I got back from my road trip. The next thing for me to do was to eat and relax. There was nothing more that I could do that day, except sit and wait.

In spite of not wanting to sleep that night, I once again fell asleep in my chair. This night I had an even worse dream. I dreamt that I was sitting on my sofa and heard someone talking to me. I turned my head to see who it was. The house was dark, but the person speaking to me was standing in some light, saying, "Travis ... Travis ... it is your sister, Trinity. I came back to get you. Why did you kill me? I was your sister. Come with me, Travis. We can be together forever."

"Trinity, I didn't kill you. I can't go with you. Leave me alone!"

Then, once again I woke up, sweating, and was still talking in my sleep. This is when I knew that I had to do something I really didn't want to do, and that was to go back to the cemetery alone and to the grave of my dead sister.

—5—

CRAZY OR TRICKED

In the morning, I was more tired than I had ever been. It had been many days since I had enjoyed a restful sleep, and the dreams were unbearable.

I knew that I hadn't killed Trinity. Why I'd had a dream like that was very unsettling. I felt like Trinity was trying to convey a message to me from the grave. In the dream she was wearing the same white dress that the woman who was tapping on my window had been wearing. I knew I hadn't lost my mind, but I was afraid that when I told this story to my father, he would think that I had.

Mother had no knowledge of the necklace, and all I could hope for was that someone did. I didn't believe in ghosts, but I began to think there was someone out there who wanted me to.

That day I got a call from the man at the jewelry store, telling me that the locket could not be opened safely. The substance that had been used on it, to glue it shut, was something that was made twenty-one years ago, and in order to open it I would need to break it. This was nothing I wanted to do just yet.

Then my phone rang and it was Aunt Mary, who told me that my father had come back to town a day early. She gave me his address, and then I was on my way to see him. For some reason, things were happening quickly.

It took me a couple of hours to get to Greenburo. It was a smaller town than Westport, and so much easier to find his home. After parking my car, I walked to the front door. I rang the doorbell and he answered.

"Travis, I didn't expect to see you for a while. Come in," Father said.

"Thank you. I got your address from Aunt Mary. I need to talk to you about a few things that have happened since the day of Trinity's funeral," I said.

"Look, Travis, I am sorry if I didn't act the way you thought I should have at the cemetery. I have had years of hurt going on inside of me, not being able to see her like I wanted to, and because of this, bitterness set in ... and sadness," he commented.

"The reason why I came here today is to let you know that I think someone is either trying to kill me or to make me think that I am crazy. The day of the funeral I went back to my office. I was going through my emails when I came to one that said '*We didn't have much time together. I will be coming back to get you.*' This was an odd message.

"Then I replied back, asking who I was talking to, and the message came back to me, saying that I had sent it to an email address that didn't exist. This was weird, but for days I tried to analyze it as to maybe it was sent to the wrong person.

"The day I left to meet my friend at the lake house, to do some fishing for a few days, I found a necklace hanging on my rear-view mirror which had a locket on it. I thought it came from Mother putting it there on her way out of town to visit Aunt Mary, but since then, after speaking to her, she says that she knows nothing about it.

"I found a black dead rose laying in the middle of my desk at work. My receptionist knew nothing about it.

"The day that my friend and I left the lake house in separate cars, I almost died. My brakes had been tampered with, and I had to drive off the highway to keep from involving other people in an accident. My insurance company told me that was what they had found out from the man who checked my car out after the accident.

"The other day at work, the elevator was stuck between floors for a couple of hours with me wondering if I was going to go crashing down to the lower floor beneath me.

"I was awakened with a tap at my living room window one night when I fell asleep in my chair. I saw a glimpse of her and she had long blonde hair like Trinity's, and a white dress on. The best I could tell was that she had anger in her eyes. By the time I got out of the front door to find her, she was gone.

"For several nights I have had horrible nightmares that make me not want to sleep. I stay awake as long as I can and then I doze off to yet another nightmare. My mind and my life is very unsettled, and I need answers!" I said.

"Wow! I am sorry, son! Someone has really been messing with you. I know that since you were a little boy, you never liked going to the cemetery. You always were afraid. That has nothing to do with someone tampering with your brakes, though.

"As for the dead rose, I think someone was messing with you. A dead person can't talk, or let alone put a dead rose on a desk. Anyone can buy a blonde long wig and a white dress. In the dark it is hard to tell who the person is.

"Elevators get stuck frequently, and this time it happened to you at a bad time, with everything else going on.

"You are probably right with the email going to the wrong person. As for the necklace, Travis, I am sure if your mother did this, she would have told you the truth.

"I am sorry for all of your nightmares. Yes, your mind is unsettled right now, but I don't think you are crazy," Father said.

"Thank you, Father. I was hoping you would say this. The brakes being tampered with has me the most concerned. I need to try to find the person who did this, and maybe by me knowing who this person is will lead me to other questions being answered. I feel like there is a clue behind the locket, but it is stuck and the jeweler said that in order to get it open, it needs to be broken. I am not ready to do this quite yet," I responded.

"Do what you think is best, but remember that you can't keep going on being tired and consumed with this. Things have a way of working themselves out," Father remarked.

"Okay, Father. I have a couple more stops to make in the next day or two. I will catch you up on all of this when I find some answers. Thank you for listening to me," I said.

"You will always be my son, Travis. I will always care about you. Be careful," Father said.

"I will."

I hugged Father goodbye and then walked out his door. One thing for sure, he had no clue about the locket either. There was a reason for it being put there, along with all the other creepy things that had taken place. I had forgotten to mention to Father about the person at the lake with the binoculars. He probably would have told me that the person was a bird watcher, or something else, just to calm me down.

That night, instead of driving all the way back to my home, I chose to eat out at a nice restaurant and get a room at a motel. I was trying to save some of my sanity, in order to continue moving forward. There is nothing better than a change of scenery.

In the morning I was going to pay a visit to the cemetery in Woodberry and also visit Trinity's mother. I still felt that maybe, some way, Trinity was trying to relay a message to me in my dreams. Father was right as I don't like the thought of death, cemeteries or anything related to them, but I had to force myself to get over this fear.

I was right, as my inner self felt protected being in a different place. I not only ate a great meal at the restaurant, but also, finally, after many nights of barely any sleep, I slept well. In fact, I didn't want to leave the motel, but there were still questions in my mind.

Before I paid a visit to Trinity's mother, I had to stop at the jewelry store and get the locket. I wasn't sure how she would fit into this, but I needed to make sure first. If, for some reason, she was the one that had hung it on my rear-view mirror, it might have been a gift from her to me, with perhaps a picture inside of her and Trinity, and I wasn't going to destroy the locket before I had a chance to speak to her.

The jeweler had cleaned the outside for me, and told me again that he was sorry he couldn't get it opened. He didn't want to damage it. I told him I understood.

My next stop was to drive back to Woodberry and see if Trinity's mother was home. This took a couple of hours and then I was pulling my car into her driveway. I walked to her front door and knocked several times. She wasn't home, so I left. It would be another day of waiting at my house before I would go back.

That night I just kept staring at the walls, asking myself what was next. I had a week of a whirlwind and until it was all over, it would continue to be much of the same, or worse. I decided to call Nick, just to let him know that I was still alive and what the insurance company had said about my car.

"Hello," Nick answered.

"Nick, my friend, I just wanted to let you know that my car got trashed. Someone tampered with my brakes," I said.

"I am sorry, Travis. Did you notify the police?"

"Not yet. I am doing some investigating of my own first. That is the main reason why I took some time off of work. I have been on the highway more than not, talking to many people who might be able to give me the answers that I need. I just wanted to call you and let you know what the insurance company found out as I thought you might be wondering," I said.

"I'm happy you did call me. I have been wondering what the reason was for you to take off work right now. Stay safe, my friend," Nick replied.

"I will," I told him.

After the conversation, I went upstairs to take a warm

bath. My nerves were still tense and I had to relax in order to sleep tonight. When I opened my bathroom door, I saw a bathtub filled with bloody water. That was not there before I left, and to me it was a sign that someone wanted me dead. I had no proof that I didn't put it there myself, and knew that the police would write a report on it and that would be as far as it would go.

So I drained the water, then packed a bag and left my house. I wasn't going to spend another night there until all of this mystery was completely solved. Sooner or later, the person doing this to me would make a mistake, and then I would know who the person was.

My living room window was open enough to where someone could get into my house, so I went around before I left and locked the windows. Instead of walking out the locked door, I ran.

That night, once again, was a night spent in a motel room far enough from my house, where I felt safe.

—6—

THE TRUTH FINALLY KNOWN

Again I sat there, thinking. The thought of someone coming into my home when I wasn't there reinforced the fact that there was a person out there who wanted to either kill me or do bodily harm. I would not be going back until whoever this person was had been captured and was behind bars at the police station.

Unfortunately, even though Nick was my best friend, I was wondering if *he* was the one doing this. Why he would turn on me was another question eating at me inside. He was with me at the lake. He sped away from the lake house, leaving me in the dust. He worked at the same building that I did, for the same company. He had the opportunity to place the rose on my desk without drawing suspicion from anyone. He knew that I was going to Trinity's funeral and also knew I would be gone for a while.

He also knew my email address. The locket on the mirror could have come from him, to make it look like someone was either giving me a gift or messing with me. It didn't take much effort to put on a dress, a wig, and stand outside a window, waiting for the right moment to tap on the glass. He also had a key to my house, in case of an emergency, and could have gotten blood from packages of meat to place in the bath water, to make it look like I was in danger.

I hated the thoughts I was having now. I had known Nick

my entire life, and because of all the many things that had driven me to this point in my mind, I had to consider anyone and everyone that I knew. If something happened to me, he would gain a better position with the company, and more pay.

For now, I had two others to go to before I went to him with this, one being Trinity's mom's home, and then the cemetery. I was hoping that it turned out to be anyone but my best friend, Nick.

I had dressed, drank coffee, and was on my way to talk to the owner of the cemetery. I wanted to make sure that it was all right if I went in there to pay my respects to my half-sister. If they had, or were, about to have a funeral there today, I didn't want to interfere.

When I got there, the man I was looking for was sitting at his desk.

"Hello. I came to pay respects to my half-sister that passed away around a week ago. Would it be all right if I go to her grave for a short time?" I asked.

"I remember you. This grave is that of a young woman by the name of Trinity Austin. Right now I will take you there, if you still want to go, but there are some things you need to be aware of first," he replied.

"Okay. What things?" I asked.

"A day after the burial, my helper went to her grave to place sod on top of it. When he got there, he just about jumped out of his skin.

"The dirt that was placed there had been dug up again by hand, and there was a hole in her casket that was very large. As you know, her mother requested a pine box for her to be buried in. Whoever it was, chopped a huge hole as it appeared that someone was looking for something that might have been placed there in her casket that might be of value, and also they took her body as well.

"This frightened the living daylights out of the grave digger. He came running back here, white as a sheet. The body was supposed to be there, and he kept shaking and saying, 'She clawed her way out of there! The wood from the pine box was shattered in places!'

"I told him that wasn't possible as she was dead when we buried her, but he refused to go back there, and so he quit.

"I had to see this for myself, so I walked to her grave. Whoever had done this had shoveled all of the dirt away from the box and had dragged her out.

"I notified the police and since then they have been patrolling the cemetery several times a night. In the process of dragging her body out of the casket and across the dirt, it was very noticeable, but not so much on the grass next to the graves around her.

"Her mother was notified immediately about this incident and was asked a lot of questions by the police. I have no idea what she told them that day, but if it was *my* daughter that all of this happened to, I would really be upset and mad.

"So far, I haven't heard anything back on whether they have found Trinity's body, and maybe checking it for prints. I know that you are her half-brother, and I will take you there if you still want to go see what her grave looks like, and how torn up the top of her casket is," the man said.

"OMG!! This was nothing that I could have ever imagined in my life! Yes, I would like to go there and see what someone did to her burial resting site," I replied.

My fear of being in a cemetery was once again coming back to haunt me. Somehow I had to find a way to get over it. The man and I walked to the grave and I saw something that I didn't think I would see beside the empty casket, and the destruction to it. I saw a black dead rose laying on the tombstone under Trinity's name.

I stood there, staring at it for a while, and at the grave. My mind was really going in circles now and wondering what someone would have to gain by destroying the casket and taking Trinity's body. Then I remembered the woman at my window, dressed in a white dress. Trinity had worn a white dress the day of her funeral. Also, the long blonde hair just like Trinity had. I was terrified!

Was it possible that the grave digger was right and she was still alive and was not the same way that she was before, because of lack of air under the ground? Could she be the one who had tried to hurt me all along? I thanked the owner of the cemetery and told him that I was also hoping that her body got returned soon and that the police could find the person who had done this sick and insane act to my sister and her grave. He agreed, and I walked back to my car.

Now, more than any other time, was the right time to go and see her mother. If she wasn't there, I would ask neighbors where she was or I would be looking for her as well. I had heard of grave robbers looking for jewelry, but nothing this horrific before today.

Within half an hour I was once again driving into her mother's driveway. I walked to the front door and knocked. This time she was home and did answer the door.

"Travis, what brings you here?" she asked.

"I just came from the cemetery and saw Trinity's grave site. The owner of the cemetery told me what they found and took me to see it. He also said that the police are involved," I said.

"Yes, they are," she said.

At that time, I took the necklace with the locket from my pocket and held it in my hand.

"I want you to look closely at what I have in my hand and let me know if you have ever seen it before," I said as I opened my hand to show her what I was talking about.

"How did you get this? It was on Trinity when she was buried!" she commented as she took it from me.

"I found it hanging on the rear-view mirror in my car the day after the funeral. I asked my mother if she had put it there, and also my father. Neither one of them had seen it before. I tried to open the locket, to see if there were pictures in it, in order to find out who it might belong to, and it is glued shut. When I took it to a jeweler to have him open it, he said that he couldn't as the glue used was something that they had twenty-one years ago.

"The day I found the necklace, I was on my way to my lake house to go fishing with a friend of mine. Within days I had several things happen to me. The first one was a strange email that came to me, and when I replied back, I got it back, stating that there was no email address to respond back to. Then the necklace that no one could identify, then my brakes on my car being tampered with at the lake. Then, I assume there was a man watching my friend and I with binoculars, and a dead rose that turned black laying on my desk at work, plus an elevator door that wouldn't open for hours when I was inside of it between floors, and then a woman in early morning hours that resembled Trinity in a white dress, staring at me with angry eyes through my glass window, and a bath tub full of bloody water.

"For many nights I have had horrible nightmares every time I fall asleep. With the blood in the bath tub and the tampering with my brakes, causing me to crash my car, was all that I needed to know that someone wants me dead as well. If you know anyone capable of doing this to Trinity, or to me, *please* tell me who it could be!" I said.

At this time, Trinity's mother started crying and I felt badly for her. She was either hiding something that she didn't want to tell me or she knew more than she had let on.

"I'm sorry! I didn't mean to make you cry. I just need answers and we need to find out who took Trinity's body so that she can be laid to rest," I said to her.

"It isn't your fault. I have been holding back tears for days now. I have the right glue removal that will allow me to open the locket. Then I will show you the pictures that it contains," she replied.

I sat there and watched her as she put this on the outside of the locket. At that moment she opened it.

"I have something to tell you, Travis, that has been kept secret for twenty-one years. It also concerns your father, and I should have told him the truth back then.

"When I found out that I was pregnant, I kept something from him. The pictures that I am going to show you are the reason why I chose to keep quiet. The day of Trinity's funeral, I placed this locket around her neck, thinking that the secret would go to the grave with her.

"The picture on the left is a picture of Trinity, and the baby picture on the right is a picture of her twin sister, Destiny.

"When they were born, I made sure that your father wasn't at the hospital. I knew for several months that instead of having one baby, I would be having two. Back then I was very poor and I knew that I could only raise one child. I wasn't going to ask your father for a dime to help me. At birth, Destiny was given to my sister to raise. At that time I was very mad at your father as he had cheated on me, just like he did with your mother. All I have wanted to do for years was hurt him as deeply as he did me.

"Trinity didn't know that she had a twin sister, but Destiny did know. My sister told her a few years ago about her when she was older. Destiny never did understand why she had to be raised by my sister instead of by me. Jealousy set in with her, and when Trinity turned 21 and got the huge trust fund from your father, just like the one you received when you came of age, Destiny became very bitter and evil, as she too wanted money.

"At that time she started playing tricks on Trinity, to make her think that she was losing her mind, just like I believe she did with you. She would hide in the shadows and scare her through a mirror that wasn't there, telling her to kill herself as no one cared. Not even me.

"Then, when Trinity found you, and was looking for her father, she was happy and wanted to know both of you. Destiny found out about this and your name from my sister. She knew that she couldn't go to her father as no one knew where he was. She wanted money, just like you got and Trinity. When things started getting harder and harder for her, she became even more evil.

"Destiny was a bigger baby than Trinity was at birth and as a child growing up. In school she took auto mechanics and knew a lot about how to assemble and disassemble a vehicle, which makes me wonder if she is the one who tampered with your brakes.

"With the dead rose that was placed on your desk, I am sure that she put it there to let you know that soon she would be coming after you, like she did Trinity.

"She was at Trinity's funeral, but went there dressed as a man in order not to be seen by me. But her being my daughter, I did recognize her, just didn't talk to her.

"The truth had to come out and, unfortunately, it didn't come out soon enough, and I am blaming myself for maybe being a part of Trinity's death as, you see, I believe that Destiny stabbed and killed her sister, and then was going after you as well.

"I kept hoping that the police would find a different person who would confess to the murder, and that it wouldn't be my only live child that I have left. I know that I need to call the police and tell them this story, so that they can find Destiny and check her home, to see if she is the one hiding Trinity's body," she responded, sobbing.

"Yes, you do, and also you need to tell my father the truth as he has a right to know all of this," I replied.

I held her as she broke down again in tears. She wasn't just losing one daughter. If I was right, she would be losing both of them, just in different ways. She had kept this secret from people that counted and had every right to know about the two babies instead of just one.

When she was done crying, she picked up the phone and made her call to the police. I stayed with her to be there when she told them the same story that she had just told me.

When Destiny was found inside of her home, they also found the decaying body of Trinity that was wrapped in thick layers of plastic. They also found the bloody knife that she had used to kill her sister.

Everything they needed to convict her was in her house. She didn't need to confess as the evidence showed it all.

Finally, I felt safe in my own home again. The nightmares went away, along with all of my fears.

One day I went to visit Destiny in jail. I tried talking to her, to tell her that if she had needed money, all she'd had to do was come to me and ask instead of killing her sister and trying to kill me too. All she did was sit there and stare at me with angry eyes that stared back at me through a window in my living room. Months later, she was brought to justice and would spend the rest of her life sitting behind bars, where she belonged.

As for Trinity's and Destiny's mother, she had a nervous breakdown and was taken to a mental hospital to get well for a year.

Trinity's body was returned to the cemetery and was put in a casket that my father paid for.

When Father had heard what had taken place twenty-one years ago, plus the rest of the story, he said that he would hate Trinity's and Destiny's mother for the rest of his life. He now knew that his secret daughter had killed her sister, but also said that he blamed their mother for Trinity's death. There was a part of me that did as well.

The day I returned to work, I also told Nick what happened, and he told me that the story was something out of a horror movie, where no one has a happy ending. He was right.

All of this was just another reinforcement of how a person can keep a secret for so long, and then the truth always comes out, in one form or another.

DEPRIVATION

PART II

FEAR AND WHAT IT BRINGS

—1—

WANTING TO BE NORMAL

Growing up in a small town would have been easy for most people. Lying in bed at night, listening to nothing but silence and looking out the window, seeing a full moon, would have given anyone peace and serenity. The still of the night gave me too much time to think before I finally fell asleep. What I thought about should have given me a calming effect, but instead, it led me down a dark place in my mind. Feeling this way made me wonder, when I woke up in the morning, if I was going to wake up every day wondering and dreading the next one.

My name is Angelina Guild. At the age of 6 is where I am taking you back to. At that age, and years to follow, was when I was taken on a journey that I wouldn't wish on anyone.

My parents tried hard to help me be a normal child, like the other children that lived in Rockford, Idaho. Unfortunately, this didn't work. Being an only child, I should have loved all of the attention they gave me. There were always plenty of Christmas presents under the tree for just me, and when my birthday came around, I knew I would probably get everything that any child could want. Once again, it should have helped to make me happy, but it didn't.

If someone knocked on my bedroom door, it made me

jump. The fear of not just whoever was knocking, but also the knock itself caused me none other than fear.

Just like my mother and father, I knew that there was something wrong with me. There were times as I sat in my room that I had the feeling of walls closing in on me, or spinning around me.

At the age of 6, my mother enrolled me in a public school. I only lasted a week before my parents took me out of it. It was decided by them that I would do home school. I had too many fears that haunted me inside. All of the teachers and children looked at me funny and were afraid of me. At the time, there was an older boy in school who would smile at me and try to be my friend.

When school was out for the day, I would wait outside for Mother or Father to drive there to get me. If I was standing next to another child, his or her parent would embrace them and pull them away from me. They all thought I was crazy or dangerous. After Mother saw this, she told the other parents they were wrong about me and told them how rude they were. This did no good as each day was the same until Mother walked out of the school with me after telling the principal that she would teach me what I needed to know— at home.

Sometimes the boy who wanted to be my friend would stop by the house to check on me and see if I wanted to go outside to play. Of course Mother would tell him that I was fine, but couldn't leave the house. With my parents knowing that I was different, and not normal, they were worried about other people in the town hurting me. So, for several years, I spent my life inside of our home, where they could watch me.

At times, sitting at the kitchen table, I would stare out the window to see what was outside. Sometimes I would see the boy who came to check on me staring back. He would wave at me and leave to go play somewhere else.

The year that I turned 13, my father got injured at the mill where he worked. For several months, my mother had to not just watch me but also was taking care of and helping him.

One day, from exhaustion, she passed out and my father called our family doctor. After hours of examining her and talking to them, they were forced into making a decision that they really didn't want to make.

In another town, not far from Rockford, was a psychiatric institution and school for children and adults that had mental problems such as mine. The doctor had convinced my parents that the older I became, the harder it would be for them to take care of and keep me boarded up in the house. He told them that he had seen improvements with other children who had gone there, and suggested that this was really the only way that they could help me as there were people there who specialized in and were trained to assist and teach others who were placed there everything that they needed to know about their illnesses.

That night, when Mother and Father sat me down to explain to me that soon I would be living temporarily in a different place, in a town with nice people who wouldn't harm me, but would help me, I grew afraid. I told them I would be good and not cause any problems if they would just let me stay at home in my room. With my telling them this, Mother started crying and told me that with them doing this, it wasn't a punishment and it wouldn't be forever.

I had many fears, and one of them was losing my parents. After seeing Mother cry, I agreed to go to where they had said I needed to go. Mother assured me that when the people at this place saw that I was okay, they would come get me immediately, to bring me home again. I guess this helped as, for once in my life, at the moment I felt like there was hope for me to be a normal person like everyone else.

A week had passed, and Mother and Father had made arrangements for me to go to this facility. We had things packed and in the car. Father, being in a wheelchair, told me that the trip would be too hard on him and that when he could and was better, he would come to see me. He hugged me and I felt tears on my shoulder as I bent over to hug him back.

Mother, fighting back tears, told me we needed to leave and that this wasn't going to be goodbye forever. So I climbed into the passenger seat, prepared to go to a new scary place that I would need to get used to, with people taking care of me whom I didn't know.

When we drove away, again I saw the boy standing on the sidewalk, watching us, and he waved at me with a sad look. Some way he knew that I wouldn't be coming home. I waved back to him, also with a sad look. He was the only one in the entire town who, like Mother and Father, wasn't afraid of me.

After several hours, Mother and I finally arrived at this facility, which was called Hopeful Center for Mental Well Being. There were many people, young and older, that were walking around outside the huge buildings that we saw.

Mother and I entered one building, where we were told which room we were to report to. This would be the place where Mother would tell me goodbye for now. My fear of feeling alone had returned, and it was hard for Mother to walk away from me. The Assistant Director that we saw told Mother to reassure me that everything was going to be fine, and then walk away. As hard as that would be on her, he told her she could do it. With her crying, she turned around and left the room.

I was afraid and continued to cry. The woman had a man in a white jacket come into the room. They took me to another room, where I would be until I could accept being there without my parents.

After a few days of feeling like an animal that was penned up, with different people coming in and out of it to talk to me about what I was feeling, and trying to find out what was causing me to be afraid, I was ready to accept the reality of why I was there, and accept being there.

When I did this, they took me out of that room and into a different one, where I felt more comfortable. This room didn't have bars on the windows or a door that stayed locked. I went to a large room each day, where there were others who appeared to be just like me. There, we were taught by therapists many things about fear and phobias and what they were, and how to recognize that they were depriving us of a good life and causing us nothing but deprivation.

I had turned 14 and was ready for a visit from my parents. Mother and Father showed up for the annual visit. Father was out of the wheelchair, but had to use a walker. They were as happy to see me as I was to see them.

We spent the day going over what I had learned so far, and were surrounded by others who also had visits from their family. Every parent talked to the psychiatrist, the child and the adolescent mental health therapist, and the intrinsic motivators who were in charge at the institution. We were told that all of us were making progress, but that we all had a ways to go before we could leave.

With knowing this, Mother and Father told me they would be back before long to visit me again, and told me to keep working through my problems with everyone who was placed there to help me.

This time when they told me goodbye, it was much different. I had accepted the fact that I needed to be there, and because of this there were no tears.

Each year passed quicker than the last, and now I was 18. My way of looking at things had changed, and most of the phobias and fears were gone. The facility had moved me again to a different building, where I would see more of the advanced adults who had also overcome their problems and were waiting to leave there to be out on their own. Or the ones who were going to leave and go back home.

I had moved forward, and with this came the freedom to come and go at the institution and school anytime I wanted.

All of those years I had been going to school here, and this year was my year to graduate. Across the room I had noticed a man who appeared to be my age, who was looking at me. Five years ago, I would have turned around and ran out of fear, but now I could see that he was nice looking. He had dark black hair with dimples in his chin. He smiled at me and, for the first time in my life, I smiled back.

—2—

INFATUATION OR LOVE?

I had walked to the table to pick up the papers to fill out as I was registering for my last year of school. When I turned around to walk away, I didn't see the man standing behind me and I accidentally bumped into him. My papers scattered on the floor, and he bent over to pick them up for me.

After he stood up to give them back to me, he said, "My name is Cane Baldwin. Most of the people here call me Bud."

"My name is Angelina Guild," I replied.

"Nice to meet you, Angelina. You have a very pretty name," Cane commented.

"Thank you. I like your name as well."

"I hope that we can be friends. I need to leave now, but will see you around here," Cane spoke.

I smiled and nodded at him and told him that we could be friends, and yes, we would see each other at school.

Several weeks passed and I found myself loving school, and waiting for the bell to ring as I knew that Cane would be waiting for me outside my classroom, to walk me to my next class. We had become closer. He was calling me Angie and I was calling him Bud, like everyone else.

There was a school dance that night, and I was all dressed up in the prettiest dress and ready to go. After Bud picked me up at my door, we were ready for the first school dance that I had ever been to. No one had taught me how to dance, so this night was going to be interesting.

My fear of being around a lot of people had gone away with the help of many people at the facility. When we walked, hand in hand, through the front door of the gymnasium, we were both smiling. Other girls who had noticed how attractive Bud was also stood around in a circle, pointing and talking about him. I overheard a conversation as I stood there, waiting for Bud when he went to talk to a friend of his.

"Look, Abby, isn't Bud the best-looking guy that you have ever seen?" a girl named Marla said.

"Yes, Marla. I don't know what he sees in her. If he was mine, he would want for nothing," Abby replied.

As I stood there waiting for him, I could feel myself slipping backward some. I was feeling ugly because of the words from Abby, and also I had a fear of Bud walking away and leaving me there alone.

Somehow I needed to put this out of my mind. The only way for me to do this was to confront Abby and Marla as they were the ones making me feel this way.

I turned around and walked over to them and said, "I see that you two are here alone. Where are your dates, or don't you have one? As for Bud, yes, he is very good-looking, but apparently when he saw you two, he didn't want to touch or be with either one of you, so as for you, Abby, there is nothing that you have that he wants, whereas with me he wants everything I have to give him."

Feeling confident about what I had said, I walked away. This may not have been the nicest or best thing I had ever done, but it sure made me feel good. When Bud returned, I was wearing a huge smile.

The night progressed, and when it was time to leave, we took a walk in the park not far from the school. There we sat on a park bench.

"We have talked about a lot of things since we met, Angie, but one thing we haven't talked about is why you were sent here," Bud said.

"I really don't like thinking backward now, Bud, but for

you, I will tell you everything. While growing up, I suffered from many phobias. The worst one I have endured is fear. I was afraid to be in my room or any other room. When I lay in bed, there were thoughts that haunted me. I wasn't a normal child.

"When my parents enrolled me in school, it only lasted a week as the faculty and other children thought that I was dangerous, or crazy. So from that time until I came here, I was taught at home by my parents. Our family doctor suggested this place, and because my father had gotten hurt at the mill where he works, and my mother was exhausted from taking care of both my father and me, they decided that I could get the kind of help I needed here better than what they were giving me. That was five years ago," I replied.

Because of Bud asking me why I was here, I asked him why he was here as well.

"Let's just say that when I was 12, I was abducted by my uncle, who wanted my family's money. He was extremely mean to me and would beat me. This affected my mind, and so that was the reason why, when I was found, my parents decided I should be here as well. For me, it has been six years ago," he commented. "I really like you, Angie," Bud said as he held my hand.

"I really like you as well, Bud. You might say that we have both grown in our minds here together," I replied.

"I agree," Bud spoke as he grabbed me to kiss me. I had never been kissed before, but I kissed him back.

Then, when I didn't expect it to happen, Bud put his hand on my knee. This time I felt fear. I wasn't ready for that and so I pushed him away.

"What did you do that for?" Bud asked me in a confused voice.

"I am not ready for that kind of a relationship, Bud. In fact, I am not sure when I will be," I said.

"I thought that you liked me," Bud said.

"I do, Bud, but if you want to be with me, it is going to take some time."

At that moment, Bud told me that it was late and we should go back to our rooms, and that we would talk again tomorrow. I agreed, and so he walked me home.

That night as I lay in bed, I kept thinking about what Bud had said and was afraid that because of my pushing him away, he would not want to see me again. So, feeling this way and being older, there was an additional kind of fear I was experiencing. This fear was called insecurity, and something else that I would need to overcome.

The next day Bud didn't come to get me at my room before school. Not knowing why, I walked there alone. When I had gotten to my locker, I heard him talking to a girl I hadn't ever seen before, leaning up against her locker and laughing. This fear was again a new one for me. It was jealousy. This was an emotion I didn't know I was capable of having.

I turned around and ran past him and the girl, crying, until I had gotten to a river that was close to the school. I was still very emotional when two men dressed in white found me and took me to see the Assistant Director of Behavior Health.

Another lady that was called in to talk to me was an adult mental health therapist. I had missed school that day as I was talking to both of these professionals about the emotions I had never felt before, but was feeling now that I am older. The therapist told me that what I was feeling happens to normal people all of the time, and throughout life it would probably happen to me again. Also, that what I had done and the way I responded to Bud by resisting his advances was called having self respect, and that I had done the right thing.

—3—

JEALOUSY AND A CONTROLLING MOTHER

The next day, walking down the hall to my class, one of Bud's friends stopped me in order to talk. "I have been watching you, Angie. I would like to take you out sometime, if you will go out with me," said Brad.

"That depends on where we are going, Brad. But yes, I will go out with you," I replied, seeing Bud standing at his locker, watching me.

"Okay. I will get back to you later," Brad replied.

"Sounds good," I said as I glanced at Bud, who continued to watch and listen to our conversation.

Brad left and I went through the doors of the classroom. Today, instead of paying attention to the teacher, my mind was again on Bud. When we were dating, I felt things I had never felt before, and they weren't going away. So I sat in the room, tapping my pencil lightly on my desk, thinking about him until the teacher came over to me.

"Angelina," she said, "are you all right? You are disrupting the class."

"I'm sorry, Mrs. Stone. I will stop what I am doing," I replied.

Mrs. Stone walked away and I sat there, doing my best to hear her words and pay attention to what she was teaching. After class, I picked up my books and as I left the classroom, Bud was standing there, waiting for me.

"Can we talk, Angie?" Bud asked.

"Sure, I suppose so," I replied.

"I am sorry for the way that I have been treating you. You mean a lot to me, and I guess when I got rejected the other night, I took it too personal. I am hoping that we can still be friends."

"Of course we can, Bud," I responded.

Bud held my hand and we walked to my next class. When he walked past Brad, he said, "She is my girl, and no, you won't be taking her out on a date."

Brad didn't reply back to Bud, but I was wearing a smile.

When school was over for the day, Bud came to walk me to my room. It was like it was before, and this made me happy. We continued to date and we were getting serious.

"I love you, Angie," Bud said.

"I think I love you too, Bud," I replied.

"Where do we go next in this relationship?" Bud asked.

"I am not sure, but the only direction that I can go in is to take things slow," I commented.

"If this is what you want, Angie," Bud spoke.

Everything appeared to be perfect. We had confessed our love for one another, and Bud had agreed to take things slow. At that moment, I was happier than I had ever been and I couldn't wait to tell Mother and Father about Bud when they came for the annual visit in a few days. I was sure that Bud felt the same way that I did about telling his parents about me.

The day of the visit, Bud and I were sitting in the gymnasium, waiting for our parents to show up. Knowing that his parents were rich, I was feeling another emotion, and this one was intimidation. The fear of them not liking me was also on my mind.

My parents were the first ones to arrive. As Mother and Father walked closer toward me, I saw their smiles and was excited to see them. If it wasn't for them putting me in this place, I wouldn't be where I am today and I wouldn't have met Bud.

"Mother, Father, I am so happy to see you again," I spoke, hugging them.

"Angelina, we are so happy to see you," Mother replied.

"Who is the man sitting next to you?" Father asked.

"This is Cane Baldwin. Everyone here calls him Bud. He is a very good friend of mine," I said.

"Nice to meet you," Mother said as Father shook his hand.

As we were talking, Bud saw his parents enter the room and waved at them, to show them where he was sitting.

"I am happy to see that you could make it here today," Bud said to his parents.

"We are happy to be here as well, son," Bud's father replied as his mother stood there, looking at me and my parents.

"Who do we have here?" Bud's mother asked.

"This is Angie, Mother. We are very good friends, and these are her parents, Mr. and Mrs. Guild," Bud commented.

"Oh," said Bud's mother.

Seeing Bud's mother all dressed up and looking down her nose at me and my parents made me feel uncomfortable. I was sure that it had done the same thing to Mother and Father.

"We are pleased to meet you," Father answered.

"Bud, we came here so that you could show us around the school," Mrs. Baldwin told him.

"Yes, I will do that, Mother. Right now I would like for you to sit down and get acquainted with Mr. and Mrs. Guild, and also Angie," Bud said.

"Maybe over dinner as we need to go back to our motel and change. Then you can show us the school, and we can have dinner," Mrs. Baldwin spoke, still looking at us like we were something that was stuck under her shoe.

"That works for us. Mother and I have to go to our motel, Angie, and then we will meet you back here at six o'clock for dinner," Father replied.

"That's fine, Father. I will see you and Mother later, back here at six o'clock," I said.

Mother and Father left, and so did Bud's parents. So far, I liked his father, but I didn't like his mother. She could be a problem for me if Bud and my relationship advanced further than it is now.

"I'm sorry, Angie. My mother was rude to you and your parents. With all the money that comes from oil rigs that we have, she makes it hard for anyone to like her. Father drinks to survive as she is even difficult for him to live with," Bud said as he held my hand.

"It's okay, Bud. It isn't your fault, and maybe she will actually like me and my parents before all of them leave here tomorrow sometime," I replied.

Bud left and went back to his room to change for dinner. I sat there, contemplating on what to say or do next. This was something I hadn't even been up against. It was called an "overprotective mother with money to flash in front of his face." I wasn't sure that I could compete with that. I got up from my chair and went to my room to also get ready for what I hoped was an evening of fun.

About half an hour before I expected Mother and Father, I put on the nicest dress I had and was waiting in the cafeteria for them to arrive. Bud was still gone and I didn't know whether he would return before we left to go eat. Soon after, I saw Mother and Father walking up to me again.

"Angelina, we get the feeling that the young man we met today is more than just a good friend of yours. Are we right?" Mother asked.

"Yes, Mother. We care a great deal about each other. After you left, he apologized for the way his mother behaved. I guess she has so much money that she thinks it is okay to be rude to everyone, including her own husband at times," I replied.

"Well, Mother and I already realized that she was this way, and just want you to know that we won't be rude to Cane or his family. We will be leaving tomorrow afternoon, and while we are here, we would like to see more of the school and also spend time with you and your friend, if that is going to be possible," Father commented.

By then, after Father had spoken, Bud and his parents came walking up to us. Once again, she was wearing clothes that only a family with tons of money could afford, whereas his father had on clothes that anyone could buy. This night was going to be challenging for me, and I had already realized that trying to get close to this woman wasn't going to happen.

"Angie, are you and your parents ready to go eat?" Bud asked.

"Yes, Cane. We are ready whenever you and your parents are," Father replied.

"Please call me Bud, Mr. Guild. That is what everyone here calls me, except for my parents, of course," Bud replied with a slight smile.

"Thank you, Bud. We would love to call you by your nickname," Father said as he helped Mother on with her coat.

We were ready to leave, and this was going to be a night to remember. I was thinking that in the worst way possible.

At the restaurant we all were talking except for, of course, Bud's mother. His father was explaining oil rigs to my father, and my father was explaining the work that he did at the mill. While they talked, Mother sat there, listening like Bud and I did. They really hit it off, and I could see that Bud was disappointed in the way his mother was acting.

After dinner we all said good night and our parents left. Bud walked me back to my room and said that we would try it again in the morning. I told him that would be fine and that it had been quite the day. Bud leaned over to give me a kiss and I kissed him back. After all, he said that we were in love.

That night, before I went to sleep, I lay there thinking about what it would be like if Bud and I got married someday. I could picture the frown that his mother would have on her face as Bud and I were standing at the altar, waiting to be pronounced husband wife. I could see her standing up when the minister asked if anyone there objected to the marriage. The words that she would probably say would be, "I object. This woman isn't right for my son as her and her family are poor."

Thinking about this made me smile. Years ago, this thought would have sent me to a dark place in my mind and I would have lay awake all night, but tonight it didn't happen and I was able to go right to sleep.

In the morning, when we walked to the gymnasium, our parents had already arrived.

"Good morning, you two," Father said.

"Good morning, Father and Mother," I replied.

"We are ready to see the school now, Cane," Bud's mother said.

"All right, Mother, I will take you around and show you and Father everything. Angie can show her parents the school. Maybe we can meet back here at noon for lunch," Bud commented.

"This will work for us," I told Bud.

With all of this being said, Bud and his parents went one way and we went a different way. It was for the best for everyone right now. Maybe someday, after Bud and I had been together longer, Mrs. Baldwin would be more accepting of me and my family. At least I hoped so.

That morning went fast, and at about 1:00 p.m., after Mother, Father and I had sat in the cafeteria, waiting on Bud and his parents to show up, Father announced that we should just go somewhere to eat as they were going to need to leave soon, to go back to Rockford. I agreed, and so we left to go to a place where Bud had taken me to eat that I liked.

For a brief moment we talked about Bud and me. This was something I expected, so was ready for question and answer time.

"So how long have you and Bud known each other, Angelina?" Mother asked.

"We met at the beginning of this school year. I first saw him the day of registration, before school started."

"I like the nickname he gave you. Angie is short for

Angelina ... and cute," Father replied.

"I kind of like it as well," I told Father.

"How close are you?" Mother asked.

"We think that we love each other, Mother. Bud is my first boyfriend, and so I am not sure, but taking things slow. He told me that he would do this as right now I am not sure where this relationship will lead us to," I said.

I knew that what I had said would give Mother the information she was looking for, and maybe help her and Father see that I was being a responsible young woman as well. Father could see that I was a little uncomfortable talking about Bud and me, so he said that we should probably just eat as time for their visiting me was running out and it was getting late in the afternoon.

After lunch Mother and Father took me back to the gymnasium and told me goodbye. They said they would be at the graduation, and if the school and the faculty would let me come home for winter break, they would love to have me with them for a few days. I told them I would need to see and would let them know later. They hugged me goodbye and walked away.

I sat there for a while, waiting to see if Bud and his parents would show up, and finally, after an hour of waiting, I left to go back to my room to change clothes.

A few hours later, I heard a knock on my door. When I opened it, Bud was standing there.

"I am so sorry, Angie. Father and I were all ready to meet you and your parents for lunch, and Mother announced that she was having one of her bad headaches and said that she needed to go back to their motel, and that she wanted me to come with them, so that we could talk.

"While I was there, she asked me a bunch of questions about us, and I told her that we love each other. She reminded me about how you and your parents are poor and that she and Father expected me to marry into a rich family. Father told her to keep him out of the decision as he likes you and your parents. When he said that, the argument was on between the two of them, until Father announced it was time for them to leave," Bud said.

"I am sorry that you couldn't make it, Bud. I do understand, and can see what kind of a predicament you and your father were in. I also got asked some simple questions from my mother, but nothing like what you went through," I replied.

Bud was not allowed in my room as I wasn't allowed in his, so we left to go on a walk.

We talked, held hands, smiled, and seemed to be having a good time. For me, at that moment, my life was good. That weekend I had experienced many emotions, and some fears that happen to adults. In my mind, I was finally feeling like I was a normal person.

—4—

REALITY AND A BEST FRIEND

For the next couple of months, Bud and I were practically inseparable. I felt like we were a solid couple and maybe would be together forever.

Finally, it was time for the winter break and all of the students who were graduating this year were allowed to leave for a few days.

Bud and I decided that we should go home and spend time with our parents. Bud said that he would call me every day and we could talk. I knew that when some of the people in Rockford saw me as a young adult, there would be talk around town, and no doubt it would be all about me.

The next day we were on separate buses, going to our hometowns. What I had seen five years ago, while looking out the window, hadn't changed, but for some reason it felt to me like I was looking at it for the first time.

When Mother and Father saw me step down out of the bus, there were again tears. That was the first time I had been back home since I left, and I expected there would be some things that would bring back mostly bad memories for me, but because of all the people at the mental health institute who had taught me about overcoming any fear, I was sure I could handle any thought that crossed my mind. I was a different person than I had been when I was there before.

As we walked through the door of the house, I looked around and it still looked the same. What I smelled was amazing. Mother had cooked stew for us for dinner.

After dinner I told Mother that I had to unpack my clothes and that Bud was going to call me. She said that she would bring me the phone if he did.

When I stood at my bedroom, getting ready to enter it, I had a weird feeling. Before I left, I had spent most my time in this room. With such negative thoughts from all of the fear, there was a part of me that wondered if maybe I should not go into the room at all. Remembering the words from the therapists, I knew that the thoughts I was feeling were from years ago, when I didn't know how to deal with my problems. The room didn't cause me to feel the way I did back then. *I* did.

So I opened the door and walked in. To my surprise, Mother and Father had given the room a fresh coat of paint, and I had a bigger bed to sleep in. They had changed the room from the "little girl" look to the "big girl" look, and I loved it.

I unpacked my clothes and went to the living room to sit and visit with Mother and Father.

"It is so good to have you home, Angelina," Mother said.

"I know, and I am so happy to be home with you and Father for a short time. If we can, I would like to go into town and walk through some stores and maybe go to the town park," I said.

"Yes, we can do this. Are you ready now to face the people of the town who made you feel so badly many years ago, Angelina?" Mother asked.

"I have been taught many things, Mother. One thing is that the only one who really matters is me. If these people still want to think badly of me, then they can because what they say or feel doesn't matter to me. I do," I replied.

At that moment, Father looked at Mother and smiled. They knew that they had done the right thing by letting me go. The doctor was right. They had done the best thing for me that any parents could do for their child who was suffering inside with fears that were causing different phobias.

They had given me life again since the first day that I was born.

It was late and time for us to go to bed. Bud still hadn't called. Being concerned that something might have happened to him, I told Mother that I would like to call him. She said that I could, so I took the phone into my room.

I dialed the number that Bud had given me, and after several rings a person answered.

"Hello, you have reached the Baldwin residence."

"Hello, my name is Angie Guild. I would like to speak to Cane, if I can," I said.

"I'm sorry, Cane is not here right now. He left a few hours ago, to go to a friend's house. Can I give him a message?" the woman asked.

"Yes, please tell him that I called, and ask him to call me back tomorrow. Thank you," I replied.

"I will do that," she said.

I hung up the phone, wondering why Bud hadn't called me. What I didn't know was that when the call had ended and I hung up the phone, Bud's mother told the woman I was talking to that she was under no circumstances allowed to let Cane know that I was calling him. The woman was the maid and feared losing her job, so she told Mrs. Baldwin that unless Cane called me on his own, she wouldn't say a word.

Mrs. Baldwin told the maid that she would do whatever it took to keep him from talking to me during the time he was there.

This was a conversation that I wish I had heard.

That night I kept the phone in my room and waited for a while for it to ring and be Bud calling. Finally, I went to sleep. I woke up the next morning with the sun shining through my bedroom window, and it felt good to have nice thoughts and excitement for a new day.

I left my bedroom to shower, and as I was walking to the kitchen to get a cup of coffee, I saw Father sitting at the table. He was up, and Mother was in the kitchen preparing some breakfast for us to eat.

"Would you like me to go to town today with you and Mother, Angelina?" Father asked.

"Only if you want to, Father. I am sure I will be all right. If Bud calls, please ask him to call me later," I replied.

"I will do that. It is so good to have you back home again," Father said.

"It is so good to be back here, Father. I know that it was hard for you and Mother, years ago, to let me go to that facility. You were worried and scared for me. I could see it in your eyes. Thank you, Father. You and Mother helped me more than you can imagine. Thanks to both of you, I am a normal young woman now with a whole lifetime that I am looking forward to," I said.

"It was hard for us, Angelina. You are our only child and all we have ever wanted for you is to be happy and healthy, not just in body but also in mind. I thank the doctor every time that I have gone to see him. I have told him how that place helped you, and he couldn't be happier for you," Father commented.

Mother was done cooking and we sat down to eat. After we were finished, Mother and I were on our way to town, to walk around and go in as many stores as we could.

For a couple of hours everything went good. I didn't see anyone that I had gone to school with there, or their parents. Then, when we entered a clothing store, I heard a couple of women talking behind a clothing rack.

"I can't believe that she is bringing her daughter to town. I heard that they put her in a mental institution and that she had everyone there terrified," a woman spoke.

"I heard that she tried to burn the place down," another woman replied.

By then, I had heard enough of what they were saying and turned around and yelled at the top of my lungs, "*BOO!*" I hadn't ever witnessed two women run so fast in all my life. I just stood there with Mother, laughing until we couldn't laugh any longer. This would give those gossipy old biddies something to think about and talk about that was true.

When we had walked inside the house, Mother and I were still laughing. Father, of course, wanted to know what was so funny, and when we told him what was said in the clothing store, he too was laughing so hard that he almost fell off his chair. We all agreed that those old bags had it coming.

Once Mother had gone to the bedroom to change from her nice town clothes into her around-the-house clothes, I asked Father if he had heard from Bud.

Father looked at me and said that the phone hadn't rung one time since we'd left. This was a disappointment for me, but knowing the way his mother was, I just chocked it all up to her having another one of her bad headaches and keeping him with her in whatever room, talking his ear off about how he should be with anyone with money other than him wanting to be with me.

I told Father that I would give it more time, and if I hadn't heard from him that I would try to call him later.

Father did tell me that a man that he knew for years had stopped by to see me. I guess word had really traveled about me being back in town. I told Father that if he came back, I would like to meet this man. Father said that for several months after I had left here, at times the man would stop by the house to check on me and see if I was all right. Father said that he and Mother had told him I was fine and that someday I would return to Rockford. Yesterday was the day, five years later, of my return.

After Mother and Father announced that they were tired and needed to go to bed, I once again called to talk to Bud. The phone rang three times and the same woman answered as she had last night.

"Hello, you have reached the Baldwin residence," she said.

"Hello, it is Angie Guild calling for Cane once more. Is he available to talk?" I asked.

"No, he is not back from where he went to last night. If I

see him, I will try to give him the message that you called," she replied.

Again I thanked her, and when I hung up the phone, the word "try" that she had spoken made me think. Why would she *try* to give him the message? There shouldn't be any reason why she couldn't just tell him. I was going to give it one more day and then, if I hadn't heard from him, I was going to ask to have Mother or Father take me to Bailey, where he lived.

That night I kept the phone with me in bed, waiting again for him to call me back before I fell asleep.

No phone calls during the night, and the next morning Mother and I didn't have any plans for the day. I was sitting on the porch when a tall, older version of the young boy that would come to the house to check on me and look at me through our window in the dining area, was there.

"Angelina, I don't know if you remember me, but my name is Neil Morgan. I was the young boy who used to come visit you at times," he said.

"Yes, Neil, I remember you. I waved at you a few times," I said.

"Is it all right if I sit here on the porch with you and visit for a while, or would you like to take a walk around town with me?" he asked.

"I would love to go on a walk. Let me tell my mother and father where I am going," I said.

After letting them know Neil and I were going on a walk around town, we left the house. The more we walked, the more we laughed and talked. I felt very comfortable being around him, and he didn't make me feel like I was a side show.

Neil was not ashamed to be with me, and knowing this made me feel important.

"Would you like to walk to the park?" Neil asked.

"Yes, I would. I haven't been there for a long time."

"Then that is what we will do. There is a Winter Carnival tomorrow, and I will take you, if you want to go."

"I would love to go. I have never been to one," I replied.

"Then that is what we will do. I am happy that you came back, Angelina. I missed seeing your pretty face," Neil said.

"Thank you, Neil. When you smiled at me when you saw me, I knew that you weren't afraid of me like the others. The last five years have taught me a lot about myself, and because of this I have learned to recognize what happened to me and I have learned how to fix it," I said.

"I'm glad, and you always will have me as a friend," Neil commented.

"Thank you, Neil," I responded as I once again smiled at him.

That day we walked around the park, looking at the ice sculptures that people had carved, and other things that were put there for the carnival. We even climbed the bleachers to sit and talk about many things. As I was coming down, I slipped on a step and fell forward. Neil was standing there to catch me. As he was holding me in his arms, I looked into his eyes and saw soft, caring, loving eyes looking back into mine. This was something I hadn't felt before, not even with Bud. Bud had said that I was his girl and I didn't want to complicate things. If I wasn't careful, this was what I was going to do.

Neil stood me down out of his arms and told me that he probably should take me home. He had cows and horses to feed. He was a rancher. If I wanted to, I was even told that I could come with him to the ranch, meet his mother, and ride a horse with him. All of this sounded wonderful someday, and I explained that I only had a couple of days left, and then I needed to go back to the facility until after graduation.

I told him that if I could, I would spend more time with him after the Winter Carnival tomorrow. Neil was excited and said that if I chose to do this, I had nothing to fear as it was just two old friends hanging out together. This made me feel somewhat better as I shouldn't be having the feelings inside me that I was having. After all, Bud had said that I was his girl.

As we walked back to my house, there was more laughing and talking. Neil was a great guy and a great friend.

When I walked through the door, once again I asked Mother if Bud had called. The answer was no. I then asked her if either she or Father would drive me to Bud's home so that I could see him, to make sure everything was all right, and ask him why he hadn't called me. She agreed that after dinner we would make a trip there. I told her that I wouldn't be staying with him and that I would be coming back home after a brief conversation.

We also talked about Neil and the fun day that we had together.

"Angelina, I haven't seen you smile as big as you are now as you talk about Neil. Father and I have known his family for many years. When his father passed away, Neil took over taking care of his mother and the ranch. They are very nice people. I am happy that you have Neil as a friend," Mother said.

"Me too, Mother. He is a very nice person and has never judged me for anything that has happened to me. He and I are going to the Winter Carnival tomorrow. We went to the park today and saw the ice sculptures. They were wonderful," I replied.

"I am happy that you are having fun. Many years ago, when I was your age, I was involved with a man who worked at a feed store. He was a couple of years older than I was and I was so infatuated with him and everything about him. We had dated for a couple of years and even talked about getting married. I was very young, but was so much in love that I was willing to do anything it took to keep this man happy.

"One night, when he was supposed to pick me up to take me to the movies, I waited for several hours and he didn't show up. I thought maybe he had been involved in a car accident while he was driving to get me. I went to his home, and as I was walking up the steps and down the sidewalk, I heard him and what sounded like a woman laughing inside his home. I walked over to the window and looked in it. I saw them dancing and holding each other tight. Then I saw him kiss her. My heart was broken and so I ran away, crying. Of course, this man had all kinds of lies to tell me, and I told him that my eyes didn't lie to me, and that what I saw wasn't just friendship. He walked away and I never saw nor heard from him again.

"A few years later, a tall, handsome man with dark brown hair and blue eyes that shined moved to town. I met him at the mill, where he worked. As you can see, I am talking about your father. We dated for a few years and then married. Because I recognized that the other man was just a crush and my first boyfriend, at the time I didn't really know what love was all about, until I met your father.

"We, as you know, have been very happy for forty years now. I guess the reason why I am telling you this story, Angelina, is because I know how much you are feeling for Bud. This is normal for anyone being young and having a first love in their life. Just remember that sometimes things don't always work out the way that we want them to. If things don't go good with you and Bud, I want you to know that someday another man will sweep you off your feet, just like your father did with me," Mother said.

"Thank you, Mother, for sharing this story with me. I always wondered how you and Father met. I will keep your words in my heart and not forget what you said," I responded.

Dinner was ready and as we sat there, eating, I found myself telling Father about the fun I had with Neil. I saw him wink at Mother once and at the time thought that it was just something they did.

Finally, with no call from Bud, we were on our way to see him. It took a couple of hours to get there, but as we drove up into a long driveway to a mansion on a hill, I couldn't believe what I was looking at. Bud's parents weren't just rich, they appeared to be *filthy* rich! His family reeked of money.

Mother stopped her car and I got out. This time I didn't feel the intimidation as I had felt at school, and walked to the front door and pushed the doorbell.

A woman dressed in a maid's outfit opened the door for me. "Hello, can I help you?" she asked.

"Yes, I am Angelina Guild. My mother and I drove here so I could see and speak to Cane," I replied.

"Cane is not here. He hasn't spent much time here since he came back," she said.

To my surprise, Cane's mother heard the doorbell and came to see who was at the door.

"Angelina, it is you again," she said, dismissing the maid.

"Yes, it's me. I was told that Cane isn't here," I replied.

"No, he isn't. He has been with his friend since he came back here, and I don't expect him back anytime soon. I knew you would make your way over here to try harder to get him in your clutches. Every poor woman wants a rich man. Before he came home, I contacted the school to ask questions about you. They were hesitant at first on giving out any information, but it is amazing what money can buy. I found out about your fears and all the phobias that you have, and I want you to leave my son alone. You are not good enough for him! Also, leave the property and don't come back here again ... or call. If you do, I will have you arrested for harassing us," Mrs. Baldwin said as she slammed the door in my face.

I walked away, feeling like I had been misjudged by her and I wanted to cry, but I couldn't. Mother asked what happened, and I told her what Mrs. Baldwin had said. Of course, Mother being Mother, wanted to walk back up to the door, and when Mrs. Baldwin answered it she said that Mrs. Baldwin would open the door to her fist! This was the protective side coming out of Mother and I told her that it was okay, that I would have time to talk to Bud and find out exactly what he had done on his break, and tell him about his mother and her harsh words. By then, Mother had calmed down some and so we left to go home.

That night, lying in bed, I thought about what Mrs. Baldwin had done and said. I had known all along that because my parents didn't have money, this would create a problem for Bud and myself. She would never like me or accept me into their family. Also, I was wondering why he didn't call me from his friend's house. He had promised to do this, and I felt, without a good reason why he hadn't, that he had lied to me. No one had ever done this.

I refused to not let my mind go back to a dark place, so I started thinking about Neil and all the fun that we had today and would have tomorrow. I had a couple more days in Rockford, and instead of wondering about what Bud was doing, I was going to have some fun of my own. I then cleared my mind and went to sleep.

The next morning, when I entered the kitchen, Father got up off his chair and came over to hug me. He then went to the coffee maker and brought me back a cup of coffee.

"I am sorry, Angelina, that woman spoke to you the way she did. That is what happens to a lot of people when they either marry into money or acquire it some way. I shouldn't say this, but she is what people call 'A Rich Bitch.' I have called the facility and talked to them about finding out who the person was who gave out your personal information. By law, they weren't supposed to do this. I wanted them to be aware of it so that it won't happen again," Father said.

"Thank you, Father. I doubt it will do any good as Mrs. Baldwin has a bunch of money and she can buy anything and everything. Today I am excited as Neil and I are going to the Winter Carnival and, right now, I don't care what Bud is doing. I am not going to let the Baldwins bring me down to their level," I commented.

"That's good. We may not be rich with money, but we have a bunch of love in our family," Father said with a smile.

It finally was time for Neil to come here to get me. I heard a knock on the door and went to answer it. Neil was there, dressed up with a western hat and western boots. He looked very handsome.

"Come in, Neil," I said.

"Angelina, you look very pretty today. How are you, Mrs. and Mr. Guild?" Neil asked.

"It is good to see you again, Neil. We have thought about

you and your mother quite often, and hope that she is doing okay. I hear that you and Angelina have a Winter Carnival to attend today, and I know that both of you are going to enjoy it," Father answered.

"My mother is doing good. She was in the hospital for a while, but is fine now. Angelina and I are going to have a great time today. There is so much there to see and do, and plenty of hot chocolate if we get cold. I will have her back before dinner," Neil replied.

"I know that you will, son. Have lots of fun," Father said.

As Neil and I walked out of my home, I was happy and smiling like I hadn't smiled before. I had found a good friend for life. In spite of the way that the Baldwins lived, I knew that their money couldn't buy them happiness. Also, that old bat's face would crack if she even tried to smile, and I wondered why Bud's father had put up with her for as many years as he had. Today I was feeling more normal than I had ever felt before, and it felt good.

Neil and I walked and talked, just like we did the other day. He could see that I had forgotten gloves, so he asked if it was all right with me if he held my hand to keep it warm. He said that when we got to a store, he would buy me a pair. I told him yes, that he could hold my hand.

At that time we stopped walking, and he took both of my hands and stood there, rubbing them and blowing on them, to help warm them up. Again, I could see how respectful and caring he was. When we arrived at a clothing store, he let me pick out the gloves that I wanted. After putting them on, I did something I knew that he didn't expect. I reached over and grabbed his hand to hold. For some reason, this was something that I wanted to do.

We continued to walk and talk, and at the park we looked at not just ice sculptures, but snow carvings. The snow had been trucked in for those who carved frozen ice. There was an ice skating rink that the town had set up as well, and so we spent several hours on it. I had never skated before, but Neil hung onto me and was prepared to catch me before I hit the ice. Just like the other day, when I tripped on the bottom step as we were walking down off of the bleachers. We had plenty of hot chocolate and a snowball fight as well.

By the end of the day, I was excited for tomorrow. Neil had asked me to join him and his mother at the ranch for the day. He said that I wouldn't be disappointed in anything that I saw or did there. I told him that I would love to spend the day with them, and that I would wait again for him to arrive in the morning. We had returned to my home and, like he had told Father, he had me back before dinner.

When I entered the house, this time I didn't ask if Bud had called. After the visit to his house and the encounter with his mother, it didn't matter to me anymore.

"Did you and Neil have fun?" Father asked.

"Yes, we did. We saw ice sculptures, snow carvings, and I even kind of learned how to ice skate. At times Neil had to catch me before I fell. It was a wonderful day. Tomorrow I will be going to his home for the day, to meet his mother and see their ranch. I am excited," I said.

"I'm excited for you. It sounds like you and Neil are becoming good friends."

"Yes, Father, we are. I have enjoyed this visit with you and Mother so much, and also getting to know Neil. I feel like we are going to be friends for life," I replied.

"I am happy that you are friends with him. He and his family have always been kind to Mother and me. One year when the mill shut down for a while, times were tough for us. At that time, I think you were around two years old. We were struggling, and Neil's father and mother gave us meat and milk from the cows, and also other animals that were butchered. This was when we really got to know them. Neil reminds me of his father. He was always a stand-up kind of man his whole life," Father commented.

"Wow, I have learned a lot about earlier years from you and Mother this visit. I can't wait to hear more stories."

That night, Father, Mother and I stayed up later, so that we could play a board game. This was the first time we had ever done this, and the first time that I had ever played a board game. My life had changed so much and I still had so much life to look forward to.

I had one more day before leaving to return to school. It was morning and I was waiting for Neil to pick me up. Once again, he was on time and wearing his western hat and western boots. He looked just like the rancher that he was.

Once again, we were full of smiles as we looked at each other. I was looking forward to meeting his mother and seeing the ranch.

As we drove there, Neil took many back roads, to show me the land that he and his mother owned. I saw all of their livestock and the horses. The day was going great, and soon we would be arriving at their family ranch home.

Neil, being the gentleman that he was, came around and opened my car door for me, just like he had done at my parents' home. When we entered the house, I could see that the living room was very large. There was a bear skin rug hanging on the wall and elk horns. The decor was surrounded with country furniture. His mother came in from another room. She had silver hair and wasn't very tall. When she saw me, she immediately smiled at me.

"Angelina, I haven't seen you since you were a baby," she said.

"It is nice to meet you, Mrs. Morgan. My parents speak highly of you and your family, and send their regards," I said.

"Would you like to sit down and have some coffee before Neil takes you around the ranch?" she asked.

"Sure, I would love it, and thank you," I replied.

Again I was feeling comfortable in their home and happy to spend time with Mrs. Morgan.

"Neil told me that you will be going back to school tomorrow. Maybe next time you come to visit your parents, you will be able to stay longer," she said.

"I plan to. I graduate in a few months and then will be able to leave there."

"My husband and I have been friends with your parents for many years. We have talked about a lot of things and shared stories of our family with each other. I just want you to know, Angelina, that I have known for years about you needing to go to the mental institute to get well. That didn't bother me at all, and we are very happy for you and proud of your parents for sending you there to get the help you needed. I thought it would be okay for me to make you aware of my knowing about you, in order to take the edge off, because I want you to come here as often as you want to, and to always feel comfortable when you are around me," Mrs. Morgan commented.

"Thank you for telling me this. I wasn't sure if Mother and Father had shared this with you, and just so you know, I felt comfortable the minute I walked through your door," I said.

This kind old woman had accepted me for who I was, and am today. I knew that she, like Neil, would be a very good friend of mine for life.

After Neil's mother and I drank our coffee, talked and laughed about many things, Neil told me that he was ready to show me around. I told him that I was ready to see whatever he had to show me and wanted to.

The first place we went to was a hill that overlooked the ranch. Neil wanted to show me how pretty it looked in the winter, with the surrounding hills. We sat there, and the beauty of it in my mind was like a wintry scenic card that anyone could buy at a store. The view was gorgeous and the hills were very pretty with the snow glistening. I could see why Neil wanted to show me this.

When we left there, we went to the barn, where he grabbed a saddle.

"Angelina, what do you think about learning how to ride a horse today?" he asked.

"I would love to, Neil. This could be comical ... and interesting," I replied.

"You will do fine," Neil said.

We walked over to a horse that he had already tied up to a fence. The horse was beautiful and seemed kind enough. After putting a saddle on it, he said that today we would take things slow.

He showed me how to get on the horse, and also told me what to do to make the horse go in the direction I wanted it to. Everything seemed to be simple enough. I was wondering if the horse was as ready for me as I was for it.

He said to hang onto the saddle horn and he would walk the horse until I could get used to being on it. Of course, I didn't know what that was and needed his assistance again.

As the horse and I started moving, I was hanging on for dear life, just in case the horse decided to walk faster or run.

When I had mastered this, Neil told me that there was something called riding a horse bareback. He helped me down and told me to hold the reins while he took the saddle off and put it on the wooden fence. I was somewhat skeptical of doing this. When Neil walked away, I was standing there, saying, "Stay, horsey, stay." With my doing this, Neil really started laughing and told me that I was doing fine.

Neil climbed on the horse, which had no saddle, and then pulled me up to sit in front of him. He was holding onto me just to make sure I didn't slip off of it some way. I was sitting on a horse, riding it with my best friend.

As we were riding, I glanced back at Neil. He looked into my eyes again and I continued to look into his. At that moment, he kissed me very softly on the lips. Then he told me that he hoped that what he had just done was all right.

I hadn't felt the need to tell him about Bud, but because of the kiss, it was something that I now needed to do.

—5—

TRUTH AND REALITIES

"Neil, if we can stop riding for a little while, I need to tell you something that I haven't told you," I said.

"Sure, Angelina, we can do that," Neil responded.

We stopped and Neil climbed off the horse. Then he lifted me off of it.

"When I went in to register this year for my last year of school, I saw a young man around my age. We started talking and before long we were boyfriend and girlfriend. The more we saw each other, the more attached we became to each other. One day, when we were walking after a school dance, we stopped in the park to sit on a park bench. He kissed me for the first time, and I kissed him back. After the kiss, he wanted more from me. He put his hand on my knee and I told him no, that I wasn't ready for that kind of a relationship right now.

"I thought he understood, but the next day I saw him talking to a different girl, and then the next day some other girl. This continued for a while, and then when his best friend asked me out, the man I had been dating saw this, and it made him jealous. He told me that he was sorry for the way he had acted and that he wanted to go back to the way we were before. I told him that we could, and so we were together for months before I came here.

"He went home to his parents' house. The other day I went to his home to find out why he hadn't called me, and was told that he hadn't been back there since the night he came in on the bus. I didn't understand why he lied to me, telling me that he would call, and didn't. I had met you, and felt comfortable being with you and talking. We were having fun walking around town and the Winter Carnival was fabulous. Today has been as well. I have enjoyed every place we went and also everything that we did. Plus, I really like your mother, and understand why my parents think so highly of all of you.

"I won't lie to you, Neil. When you look into my eyes, I have a feeling inside that I haven't ever felt before, but because of the man from school, I feel like I need to talk to him and give him the opportunity to explain why he didn't call me as he promised, and ask him why he chose to spend day and night with his friend. I have learned many things at this school and facility, and one of them is honesty and the other one is integrity. So, because I didn't expect you to kiss me when you did, I felt like it was time for me to share this part of my life with you. Our time that we have spent here together has been precious to me. I finally found a friend that I can share things with and feel comfortable being around. In other words, you mean the world to me, but before I can open another door, I need to close this one. This is the only way that I know how to explain it to you," I replied, wondering what Neil would say.

"Angelina, I have wanted to be your friend since the first day of school. When the others treated you badly, it hurt me to see this happening to you. I could see that your pretty face was sad, and even though I didn't understand why, I wanted you to smile and be happy. When you left, I went to your home a lot, to check on you and make sure that you were okay. I didn't do this wanting anything back in return from you. I did it because of you and the kind of person that you were and became.

"When I heard from your mother that you were coming back here for a few days, I couldn't wait to see you again and get to know you and be friends for life. Yes, I too am feeling more inside for you than I probably should be right now, and when I look in your eyes, I can tell that you are having feelings as well. The kiss was unexpected and not planned. I won't lie to you ever, and I will tell you that it was beautiful, but I won't put you in a situation where you feel uncomfortable being around me as you have a commitment that might turn into what you have dreamed about your whole life.

"Only you can decide what is in your heart and the direction that you want to take in your life. I won't be going anywhere, Angelina. I have waited five years to see you again, and I would wait twenty years if this is what it took just to be your friend, if nothing else. Our time together has been amazing, and so, forget the kiss and it happening, and when you leave here tomorrow, you do what is best for you. I just don't want to lose you as my friend," Neil responded.

When I heard his words and looked into his eyes, I could see the sincerity in them and in his voice. I believed him. His eyes were like a magnet that pulled my eyes into his.

"Okay, Neil, what are we sitting here for? Let's go have some fun on that horse," I said.

Neil smiled at me and said, "I might teach you how to be a cow girl after all."

I laughed as I was trying to get on the horse myself and, after many tries, Neil lifted me onto it. We had so much fun together, and this was something that I was going to miss when I went back to school. I knew that as soon as I graduated, I would be coming back home, either to stay or just to visit again. Depending on Bud and what he had to say for himself, I might be coming home.

At the end of the day, Neil released the horse in the pasture and we were on our way back to my home. It would be a while before we saw each other again, and I felt inside like I never wanted to say goodbye. I was having another emotion that I hadn't experienced. This one was called attachment, or maybe true love, and I was finally finding out what it really is. I wasn't sure, and knew that I had plenty of time to figure all of this out.

Neil walked me to the door and said, "I want you to stay safe, Angelina. Remember that you have a very good friend who will always care about your well being. I won't say goodbye. What I will say is 'later' to you," Neil told me as he walked away. It was time to go inside. I needed to think.

Mother and Father were waiting for me inside, to ask how my day had gone.

"Angelina, did you have fun at the ranch today? What did you think of Neil's mother?" Mother asked.

Standing there, I wanted to tell her how I was feeling in my heart right now, but chose not to. It was too soon. So I walked over to the table and sat down.

"I loved the ranch, and Neil's mother. She accepted me the minute that I walked through the door. She told me how good of friends that you have been for many years, and that you had told them where I had gone. She said that she understood and that she was proud of both of you for making the decision that you made. I, too, am proud of you," I replied.

"We knew that you would enjoy it out there. Yes, she is a lovely woman, and her husband was the salt of the earth," Father remarked.

"Neil is a wonderful man as well. He showed me the ranch from a hill that overlooked their property, and the beauty of it being a winter scene made me think of a beautiful picture card. He had a horse tied up to a wooden fence and he asked me if I wanted to learn how to ride it. I told him yes, and it was nothing but comical from that moment on. I tried riding it with a saddle, and then Neil and I rode it without one. We rode for several hours today. It was a lot of fun," I replied.

"When you return after graduation, for as long as you want to stay here, I am sure that you will have more fun and time that you will want to spend at the ranch," Mother said.

"After graduation, I am not sure what my plans are going to be right now. I will return home for a while and then I might decide to move somewhere else. I still have a lot of thinking to do. I have a few months to decide what I want to do," I remarked.

"Of course, and we understand. Tonight we have some time left in the day to sit and talk before it gets late," Father said.

Our time together that night went fast and it was time to go to bed. I had one more night at home until I would be leaving on the bus to return to the facility and school.

In the morning, Mother, Father and I were rushing around to get me to the bus station on time. Father had my suitcase and Mother and I were on our way to the car. At the bus station, the bus was on time and already loading. Father gave them my suitcase and ticket, and then once again it was an emotional goodbye. When I climbed on the bus and found my seat, I sat there, waving at them from the window.

As the bus started driving away, I saw Neil standing there, waving, wearing a sad look like the one that he had many years ago, when Mother had taken me to the institution. I smiled and waved back at him, to let him know that he would always be on my mind and be my friend, no matter where my life took me.

Within a matter of hours, I was back at the facility. I went to my room to unpack and wait to see if Bud showed up.

I still had Neil on my mind, and the sad look that was on his face when the bus drove past where he was standing.

After a few hours, I heard someone knocking. Was it Bud, or someone else? When I opened the door, standing there was Bud.

"I know that you are mad at me, Angie, for not calling you while we were away from here, and I don't blame you," Bud said.

"You are right, Bud. I asked every day if you had called and always got told that you hadn't. I don't know what your excuse is, but it had better be a good one. Did your mother tell you that I came to your home to talk to you, and what she said to me?" I replied back with a firm voice.

"The night that I got there, a friend of mine called and asked me if I wanted to hang out for a few days. I said yes, as I found that to be more appealing than staying home and listening to my mother for days at a time. I asked my friend if there was a phone, and was told that it had been turned off. When I finally did return to the house, Mother did say that you had stopped by to visit, and she had told you that she hadn't seen me for many days," Bud responded.

"Yes, I had my mother take me there, only to be insulted by her. She called the school and institute and talked to someone about why I was put in here. She said that they told her they couldn't give her that information, but like she said, her money can buy anything. She also threatened me with calling the police and charging me with harassment if I called you again, or came back. You don't know how she made me feel. My own mother was ready to go to the door, and when your mother answered, she wanted to knock her out. You should have found some place other than your friend's house to call me, Bud. You really don't have an excuse for that," I replied.

"You are right, Angie. All I can say is that I am sorry for not calling you when I said I would, and also for what my mother did. She is out of control, and even my own father leaves and is gone for days because he doesn't want to be around her," Bud said.

"Why does your father put up with this kind of behavior? He could always get a divorce from her and find someone else."

"He could, but if he did, he would be penniless. You see, Angie, my mother is the one who has the oil rigs and the money. My father gives into her so that he can continue to live a good life with the money that she gives him," Bud said.

"Well, that explains a bunch then. I still am not sure if we should be back together again, Bud. To me, you lied when you said that you would call me every day," I spoke with once again a firm voice.

"Again, I am sorry, Angie. When I told you that, I had every intention of calling you, but when I got around my old friend, it was as if I hadn't left. We had a good time, but in my mind I was thinking about you the whole time," Bud said as he was still making excuses for his actions.

"I suppose we can try it again, but it won't take much for me to call it quits with you," I said.

"Okay," Bud said.

So, Bud had told me what his excuse was. To me, it was not good enough, but I decided that I would try for the last time with him. We would see what happened next, and it wouldn't take much for me to walk away. I had found self-esteem and respect for myself, and wasn't going to give it up for anyone.

We left the room and walked around the school for a while, and then I told Bud that I was tired and needed to go to bed.

"Just so you know, Bud, I also had fun while I was at home. I went to the Winter Carnival, walked around town with Mother, and went to my friend's ranch. I learned how to ride a horse. I had the best time that I have ever had," I said as I told him good night and shut the door in his face, wanting him to think about how easy it would be for him to lose me.

I turned out the light and went to lie on my bed. As I lay there, I was thinking about Neil and missing his smile. What I didn't know was that Neil was also lying on his bed, thinking about me.

Several days had passed, and Bud and I were hanging out more together again. To me, our relationship wasn't the same as it had been before the break, when we both went home.

I had gotten a letter from Neil, telling me that he missed me and was looking forward to my return again. He told me that his mother was very sick and that he wasn't sure if she was going to make it this time. A part of me wanted to get on a bus and leave here, to go be with him, as I knew that he needed his best friend right now. But if I did go, I wouldn't graduate and would not be able to come back here again.

So I wrote him a letter, explaining that I would love to

be with him, but couldn't. About a week later, I got another one from him, letting me know that he understood and that his mother had passed away. He said that he would be fine, and that he would see me again soon.

This was awful news as I really did like her. She was nothing like Bud's mother.

Bud and I had talked many times, holding hands, and I could see that he was trying to make up for what he had done to me. But when I looked into his eyes like I had Neil's, all I saw staring back at me was a blank expression.

Many letters followed from Neil in the weeks to come, and also from my mother and father, letting me know that they were checking on Neil, to make sure he was all right. Also, that they were excited to be coming to my graduation in a few weeks.

What I didn't know was that Bud had been getting letters himself from his friend that he had hung out with when he was home.

Days passed, and the night before graduation, Bud and I had gone to the cafeteria to eat.

"I can't believe that we are graduating from this place tomorrow, Angie," Bud said.

"I will be happy to leave here," I said. "I need to go home for a while. What are your plans , Bud?"

"I will be going home as well for a while. I need to talk to my mother about how she treated you when you went there to see me," Bud replied.

"Bud, I don't know if it would ever work out for us. She will never accept me, and after the way she talked to me, I don't think I can ever accept her," I said.

"I don't know about that, Angie. I am pretty sure that after a while you two would become friends," Bud commented.

As we were sitting there talking and getting ready to walk out of there, a woman who looked like she was about 20 entered the cafeteria and started walking over to us. I could see the blood draining from Bud's face, but didn't know why.

"Bud, I need to talk to you," she told him.

"What are you doing here, Sharon? You should have stayed at home," Bud said.

"What I need to tell you is important," Sharon said.

"Whatever it is that you want to talk to me about can wait," Bud responded.

"No, it can't, Bud. I am pregnant. You are the father!" Sharon spoke.

At that time I think a little blood drained out of my face as well. When we went to our homes, it looked to me like the "friend" that Bud was hanging out with was this woman named Sharon. Years ago, this would have crushed my heart, but today I felt numb. But it was like the story that Mother had told me about her first love, and I was prepared to walk away.

"No, Sharon. There is no way that baby could be mine. I don't know what you are trying to pull here, but it isn't working. Go back home now!" Bud said loudly.

Bud kept looking at me, to see the expression on my face. I could see that he was wondering what I was going to say to him and do. I looked at Sharon's belly and there was no doubt that she was carrying a baby. Whether it was Bud's baby was still not established yet, but some man had a surprise waiting for him. If it was Bud's baby, I would love to see the look on his mother's face when he gave her the news as this girl didn't look like she had money in her family either. There was a part of me that was torn and another part of me that was relieved.

"I need you to come with me, Bud," Sharon said.

"No, Sharon. I am here with Angie, and you can see this," Bud replied.

By then, Sharon was tired of the conversation and did walk away.

"Angie, it isn't true," Bud said.

"If it is, this explains why you didn't have the time to call me when you were home."

"Yes, but it isn't true," Bud spoke.

"Right now, Bud, I am not sure what is true and what

isn't. You told me that you understood why I wanted to take our relationship slow, and I believed you, just like I did with everything that you have said to me. Now I am not sure what to believe. Tomorrow, after graduation, we can talk again, but right now I am going back to my room *alone!"* I said.

Bud had put his head down and just sat in his chair. I knew that he was watching me walk away, and he wasn't sure if it was for the last time.

The next morning, I was ready for my last day here. I would be graduating and ready for a new start anywhere but here. I knew that sitting in chairs, waiting, were my mother and father, wearing a smile along with all of the other proud parents to watch family members graduate so that they could also take them home.

When I walked into the gymnasium, I saw Mrs. Baldwin glaring at me. I nodded at her and smiled, to show her that what she felt about me didn't matter to me. I also saw Bud looking and wondering if I would believe him or continue to walk away. When we sat down in our chairs, the Assistant Director of Behavioral Health gave a speech about how all of us had excelled in school and overcome our problems, and were ready for life outside of here. The principal of the school also spoke, and then we were being called up on the stage to get our diploma.

I watched Bud walk up there and also saw Sharon sitting in a chair, waiting to talk to him again. When it was my turn, I too walked up there to receive my diploma and my ticket out of this place. I was ready and looking forward to every day, no matter what it brought or where it took me.

Graduation was over, and we all threw our caps up in the air. When I looked over at Mother and Father, I saw them clapping and cheering for me. I also saw Neil stand up, clapping and smiling at me. I stood there, looking at Bud watching me, and when he started to walk over to me, I again looked at his mother and at Sharon. I did something that no one there would ever expect.

I ran over to Neil and put my arms around him and

kissed him. Everyone in the gym again stood up, except for Mrs. Baldwin, Bud and Sharon, and clapped for us.

I was sure at that time that he was wondering how he was going to explain Sharon to his mother.

For the first time in my life, I knew that what I felt inside was pride, contentment, peace, self respect and, hopefully, true love for Neil. When I came here, I was consumed with so many fears, and with the help I had received, there was no room in my mind for fears to survive.

After the kiss, Neil, Mother, Father and I left the room to go get my things that I had brought there before we left to go home.

Bud, with a pregnant friend, had now realized that for every action there is a reaction. For me, it was walking away from him forever and looking forward to a wonderful life with my best friend, Neil. For Bud, it would be starting his life with Sharon, a baby and many years of listening to his mother try to control him. To me, his fears had just begun.

DEPRIVATION

PART III

ON THE ROAD AGAIN

—1—

MEMORIES TO A BEGINNING

As I slowly turn the steering wheel of my big rig onto the entrance ramp going east, I see another rig up ahead with a tire that looks like it could blow at any moment.

I lean forward to pick up my CB radio, to make the person driving aware of the situation before things go bad. This particular rig was not just pulling one trailer, but two.

"Hey, big buddy, I am on your back side, coming up on you quick. I'm letting you know that you have a tire ready to blow on the west side of your rig. Keep truckin' and your ears on as there could be a Smoky up ahead. Over and out."

"Thank you, good buddy. I'm pulling off at the next exit to take care of the problem. Keep truckin'," said the rig driver.

As I passed him, I blew my horn a couple of times, to show him that I was a good buddy and that I had his back as I knew he had mine, with this being the code of a trucker.

My next stop would be Memphis, to unload the big trailer that I had picked up and been hauling since I left King City, California, a week ago. After the truck was unloaded and the trailer dropped off, my next journey would take me to my aunt's house in Atlanta, where I would be until it was time to haul again on the open road. There would be lots of time for me to spend some quality hours with family and a few other people that I knew there.

My name is Kim Cross. I bet you expected me to be a man, considering that I drive a big rig from one state to another. I have gotten many looks from people standing around or walking by when I climb out of the cab. Whenever anyone thinks of a truck driver, they think of a big, hairy, gnarly looking guy weighing in at 200 pounds. Instead, I am 29 years old, 110 pounds soaking wet, and 5 foot 2 inches tall. Many people have asked me, "How do you handle that?" Of course, they are referring to my truck. When I reply back to them, my words are, "Even though I am a woman, I have had good training and I drive a safe rig that goes down the highway as easy as a car."

The sun will be down soon. I know that I need to get off the interstate. Being familiar with the area, within a short distance there is a truck stop for rigs and a nice restaurant. I started slowing down and preparing for my exit, where I would be until morning.

My truck was furnished with a fairly comfortable bed and a small fridge. Not the most comfortable accommodations, but good enough for me.

I woke up to a bright sun shining through the windshield of my cab. It was time to get dressed and make my way into the restaurant for food and coffee. When I climbed down out of my rig, there were again people who had come out of their cars, staring at me like I was some kind of a side show. So I did what I always do—just nod and smile. If they only knew what inspired me to be an over-the-road truck driver, maybe they wouldn't look so hard at me.

When I walked through the doors of the restaurant and went to a table, the waitress came over to take my order. She was short, just like me, with a pencil stuck behind her right ear. She pulled out her small note pad from her pocket and said, "What can I bring you?"

"I'll have a couple of scrambled eggs, ham, hash browns and some toast. Also a cup of hot black coffee as I still have a long drive ahead of me today," I replied back.

"Okay, I'll be back with the coffee."

"Thank you."

While sitting there, waiting for my food, I looked around the room and wondered what the story was for the other truck drivers who, like me, chose to drive a big rig.

As I looked down at the table, it took me back in time many years ago.

I have a brother and two sisters that I always admired and wanted to be a lot like. Growing up, they not only got A's in school, but excelled in everything that they always did. They were a hard act to follow as the highest grade I got in school was a B, no matter how hard I tried.

My brother Allen was very creative and outstanding in thespians when he was in high school. After he graduated, he went to Pasadena Playhouse in California, where he acted in a couple of horror plays at the school. He managed to find a good agent and also starred in several movies that me and my family went to watch at the drive-in. With hard work, he later became a movie producer.

My sister Kate, after high school, pursued a career in modeling. She was tall, slender and turned heads everywhere she went. Eventually, she became a top model for an agency in New York.

Then there is Ellen. She is the third oldest sibling that I have. Ellen is not only smart, funny and beautiful, but also the one that I feel the most comfortable going to when I need advice, or just a shoulder to cry on. When Allen and Kate left home, there was just Dad, Ellen and me living in a big house.

There were nights when we would sit in front of the television, watching a good chick flick with a box of tissues between us as we both knew that either the hero or the heroine was going to get killed at the end of the movie, but we still watched to see if maybe someone would save the day, and this wouldn't happen.

At night, when Dad would open our bedroom door and turn off the light, telling us that it was way past our bedtime, and to go to sleep, we would wait until the bedroom door closed and then we would have a pillow fight. Sometimes we would hear Dad standing outside the door, saying, "That's my two girls." We knew that he had a big smile on his face.

Ellen loved combing and braiding my hair while giving me fashion tips on how I should dress and what I should wear the next day when I went to school. I just thought that she was very knowledgeable in what the latest styles were because she looked through the different magazines that were laying around the house.

When the day came and she graduated from high school, she had talked to me about wanting to be a fashion designer. Being very talented and having a gift like Allen and Kate, I knew that she could do whatever she wanted to do and be whatever she wanted to be. She had made sketches of women wearing a beautiful dress, or something else that she created when she thought I was asleep. With what she had drawn, she took it to a fashion house. Needless to say, the people there were very impressed with her work and drawings, so they signed her into a long contract, and she was on her way to success, making tons of money every year.

After high school I wanted to believe that I would do well as an architect. So I enrolled at Colorado Mesa University. At the time, our dad was still an Army Recruiter stationed in Grand Junction, Colorado. My mother had passed away many years before I started high school. This left my dad to raise all of us alone.

The first day of school at the university, I was like every kid who faces this at a new school. I was shy and afraid. Did I mention slightly overweight? Getting run over in the halls was not on my "to do" list. With practice, I learned to dodge the bigger kids and stand at the back of the lunch line, waiting to make my way to the front, where I could buy food that day. Also learning where to kick my locker, to get it to pop open as the combination didn't work, and the maintenance man, in spite of all of his efforts to get it to work, hadn't fixed it yet.

After a couple of years going to school every day scheduled, and working part-time at a burger place to pay for school, I stood at my locker, pondering things over in my mind and rethinking my life, and what I really wanted to do. My grades were good. I had made some friends and the classes weren't totally boring to me. But there was something missing in my life.

That is when i realized that I wanted to be something great for my family, and not doing what I really wanted to do for myself. I kicked the locker one last time, retrieved all my books and personal belongings, and walked out the door of the university. This was a big wake-up call for me, realizing that I couldn't live my life for anyone but myself.

So what if I wasn't as smart or talented as my siblings? They were doing what they wanted to do, and now it was time for me to do what I really wanted to do. I remembered the time when Dad and Mom took all of us to Knott's Berry Farm. As we were driving on the interstate, my dad saw a huge rig approaching us. He said, "Look, kids, there's a giant truck."

We all turned our heads to look, and as the trucker passed us he blew his horn twice and waved at us. The feeling inside of me at that time was amazement, and I sat in the back seat, picturing myself sitting behind the steering wheel, driving that huge truck. As I stood there remembering things that had made me happy, I knew what I wanted to do with my life.

I went home and packed some of my stuff, sat down beside my father and told him what my plan was in life from that day forward. With some tears streaming down both our faces, he told me that I shouldn't let an opportunity like what I needed to do for myself pass me by. I told him not to worry about me and that I was going to be gone for a while, but would be back when I could be.

He shook his head yes with a smile, and I knew that he was giving me his blessing. I headed east to Denver, Colorado, where I signed up for truck driving school. After weeks and months of intense training, I had completed it and was done. It took me a couple of weeks to find a company willing to hire a lady trucker. It shouldn't have been like this, but it was, and I was then working for an over-the-road trucking company. They issued me my rig that I have been driving ever since.

Do I have any regrets about my decisions that I made? The answer is NO! I love traveling and being out on the open road, experiencing things that some people only dream about doing, and can't.

My days of sitting at a movie theater alone, waiting for the movie to start, eating popcorn with a tall person who insists on sitting in front of me, with me needing to raise up in my chair to be able to see the whole screen and picture, is over with. I am sure that the tall person in the seat in front of me is also happy as well, as he or she, I know, got tired of wearing popcorn home after the movie as sometimes, when I stood up to see the picture, I forgot to pick up the box from my lap that ended up stuck to their sweater. Did I mention that caramel popcorn is sticky?

What I was doing was something that I loved and wouldn't trade for any architect job.

I had finished my thoughts of my past, and was done with my food. I paid the waitress and walked out the door of the restaurant to walk across the parking lot and climb into the one thing, so far in my life, that made me happy. I started my truck and was on my way to Memphis to deliver the load and the trailer.

Several hours went by and my job was completed as I had made it to another destination without any problems and a safe trip. Before long, I would be Atlanta bound, where I knew my family was waiting for me. It would be nice to have time to rest and catch up with everything happening in my family's life. I knew that my life was going great.

—2—

FEELINGS SHARED

After a night of rest in my rig, I was up early and on my way to Atlanta. I had 383 miles to drive, and by tonight I knew I would be knocking on my aunt's door. Knowing how she is, I was certain that she would be watching out her big picture window, to see the moment that I drove into her driveway.

Aunt Betty is my mother's sister. She is the oldest of her siblings and had many stories of her own that I had heard when I was growing up. Even after my mother passed away, she would come to visit us a couple of weeks each year, to bring us gifts and spend time with us. Even though my siblings and I are grown, we still make time for her each year.

With my doing what I do for a living, at times it makes it a little harder, but when I get the opportunity, I take it. Aunt Betty and I have discussed this and she fully understands and hasn't once made me feel guilty for not spending as much time with her as my sisters and brother have.

My father retired from the Army around three years after I left home. He had spent many years serving Uncle Sam, and also wanted to travel to destinations that the military hadn't taken him to. This lasted for a while, and then a couple of years ago he got very sick, and we found out that he had only a short time to live. Within six months he passed away and God took him home. With him being the only child, and all the rest of my mother's siblings passing as well, the only one left is Aunt Betty. I guess that is why we all try to spend quality time with her as much as our jobs will allow us to.

With each road trip that I make, I experience an adventure and someday I, too, will find the perfect place to plant my roots when I retire.

After driving for five hours, I saw the exit sign that would take me to Aunt Betty's home. Like a small child, my excitement was taking my breath away. I needed a rest and I knew that there was no better place to find it than being with Aunt Betty, Allen, Marie, Rob, Kayla, Jim, Kate and Ellen.

Driving the tractor rig through Atlanta was going to be challenging, but I would take the street that was designated for delivery trucks and then a shortcut to my aunt's house.

It wasn't long and I was pulling in her drive. Like I thought, she was in the house, waiting for me to arrive. As soon as I shut down my tractor, I saw her coming out of the door with her arms wide open, waiting to hug me. She was smiling from ear to ear, just like I was.

I climbed down out of my cab and gave her my usual hug. "Aunt Betty, it is so good to see you again!"

"I know, Kim. I have been so anxious to see you as well."

"Have you heard anything from Allen, Kate and Ellen?"

"Yes, and we can go inside out of the sun and talk, dear."

We walked into her house, and it looked like she hadn't changed anything around since I last saw her. As usual, her house was spotless and organized.

I sat down on her sofa and she went to the kitchen to pour me a glass of iced tea.

When she entered the living room and handed me the tea, she said, "I talked to Allen a week ago and he will be here with his wife and kids tomorrow. Kate had a photo shoot to do today, and then she and her husband will be on a plane and arriving tomorrow as well. Ellen said that she will also be here in a couple of days, and to tell you that she has a surprise for you."

Out of all of my siblings, it was no surprise that Ellen would be the one who would do this.

"That sounds great, Aunt Betty. I can't wait to see all of them. It has been a while since we were all in the same place at the same time," I replied.

"Tell me, dear, has your life changed any since I last saw you?" Aunt Betty asked with a slight giggle.

"No. All I do is just ride from state to state in my tractor rig, pulling big loaded trailers around to wherever they are designated to go."

"Have you met any nice fellas along the way?" she asked.

"No, I am sure I have either passed them on the road or walked past some, but no, Aunt Betty, I don't have a man in my life now. I am not saying that this won't ever happen, but for now I am content just doing what I have been doing alone," I said with a slight smile as I knew that question was going to happen, as it did with every visit that I had made there.

"Well, as you truckers say, dear, keep your ears on, as you never know."

This made me laugh and I hugged her again. She was a very old woman, but still tried to fit into a younger person's life, even if she did get her conversations and words messed up.

It wasn't long and we had dinner, and then as I sat there in the living room, watching television with her, I looked over and saw that she had gone to sleep in her chair. I went to wake her up, to help her to her bedroom. She was tired and so was I. I was excited for the next couple of days as I knew that I would be seeing my family again.

When I opened my eyes the next morning, I heard Aunt Betty moving around in her kitchen and smelled bacon and knew that she was preparing a good breakfast for both of us. It had been a while since I had slept in a big bed and I wanted to lie there and enjoy it. But instead, I raised up, rubbing my eyes, and went to shower, then find something nice to wear, and get ready for everyone.

I would spend my morning helping my aunt finish up

on her preparation for Allen, his wife Marie, and their two children, Rob and Kayla. Also, the wait to go to the airport to get Kate and her husband, Jim, unless they decided to rent a car. I had a feeling that it was going to be a full day before anyone finally arrived. Whatever the case may be, I would be ready for it and so would Aunt Betty.

When I entered the kitchen, she was already putting plates and utensils on the table. She heard me showering and knew it wouldn't be long before I made an appearance.

"Good morning, Aunt Betty," I said.

"Good morning, Kim. How did you sleep?" she asked.

"Very well, thank you. Your bed here is much softer than the one in my rig, and I miss that when I am on the open road," I replied.

"After breakfast we are going to the store. I need to pick up a few things that I forgot to get the other day. This will give me a chance to show you more of Atlanta that you haven't seen from the truck route," she added.

"That would be fun, Aunt Betty. I would love that."

During breakfast we chatted some more, and she told me about the neighbors who had moved in across the street and their dog. She loved the new neighbors, but not so much their dog as he had dug up her flower bed. One thing I knew for sure was that with every trip here, Aunt Betty managed to make me laugh with all the stories she had to tell.

As I sat across the table from her, I looked at her face, hair, build and watched her as she used her hands when she sometimes talked. It made me think about my own mother and wondering if she had lived, if this is what she would have looked like today. Maybe this is why all of us love spending time with her as it is a picture in our minds of our wonderful mother who passed away too soon.

We had finished breakfast and the dishes were done. It was time to make a quick trip to the grocery store before Allen and his family arrived. Aunt Betty kept her car in the garage and in perfect condition by keeping it out of the sun. She was very proud of it and I was very proud of her.

On our way to the store, we talked some more. She showed me parts of the beautiful city of Atlanta and told me that there were many new buildings that had been built in the last year. She also told me that she hoped I would consider Atlanta to be where I put down my roots when I got tired of being a truck driver. She even threw in that there were a lot of handsome, available men who lived there, and that maybe I should start looking for a lifetime partner.

She said that she was about my age when she had found Uncle Henry, and that time goes by too quickly, and not to waste a moment of it. All I could do was smile at her and shake my head yes. She was probably right, but right now I had a bunch of living to do and I wasn't ready to settle down with anyone. I did tell her that I would give it some thought, though. That seemed to pacify her, and so we moved on to the next conversation.

It was a quick trip into the grocery store, and then we were on our way back to her home. Aunt Betty had made another pitcher of iced tea and was prepared for lots of company. So was I.

As we sat and talked some more, I heard a car pull up in her driveway. We both went to the window and saw Allen, Marie and their two children climb out of a fancy sports car that I knew would take me my whole lifetime to save for.

We went to the door and stepped outside to greet them.

"Allen, Marie, it is so good to see you again," Aunt Betty said.

"It is so good to see you too, Aunt Betty, and how are you doing, Kim? It is good to see you as well," Allen replied.

Again we went inside so that Aunt Betty could go to the kitchen and bring them a tall glass of iced tea as well.

"Seriously, Kim, how are you doing?" Allen asked.

"I am doing really good. Right now I am on a two-week break from my over-the-road hauling of trailers that are delivered loaded, and as usual, I wanted to come here to be with all of you for a well needed visit. We don't seem to keep in touch anymore, like we used to. How have you been and how is the family?"

"We also are doing good. I have a new picture that will be out in December, just before Christmas. Marie is doing good with her paintings and the kids are excelling in school. Rob just got an award for his science project, and Kayla just got nominated class president by her classmates at school.

"I am also anxious to see Kate, Jim and Ellen. I got a message telling me that Ellen has a surprise for me, and I am anxious to know what it is. I ask as I am one that doesn't like surprises. She wouldn't tell me what she is surprising us all with, and told me to exercise some patience. I laughed when she told me this as back in the day, when we were growing up, Ellen was the one that had no patience." Allen chuckled.

"I know as I am anxious to find out what it is as I got the same message from Aunt Betty. It sounds like you, Marie, Rob and Kayla are doing great, and I couldn't be happier for all of you," I replied.

By then, Aunt Betty was back with the tea and had sat down to ask her own questions and add to the conversation. It was so good to see my big brother again and his family. They all looked very happy, and Allen and Marie were just as close as ever. Even after many years of marriage, they still couldn't keep from touching each other or holding hands.

It was getting later in the day and we heard a knock at the door. When Aunt Betty opened it, we all saw Kate and Jim standing on the doorstep. We had all been so busy talking that we hadn't heard the car they had rented drive up.

"Oh my," Aunt Betty said when she opened the front door. "We would have picked you up at the airport if we knew you were there."

"It's okay, Aunt Betty, we wanted to rent a car anyway. We are so happy to see all of you again," Kate said as she handed Jim her jacket to take care of for her.

"It is great seeing you and Jim again," Allen said as he hugged Kate and shook Jim's hand.

"Kim, how have you been?" Kate asked.

"I have been fine. As you can see, I am still driving a big rig across country, and loving it," I replied.

"I was a little shocked when I heard from Dad that you had given up on becoming an architect. All of us went for the gold, and it seemed like you gave in to a meaningless life that I am sure doesn't pay that much. Not that it is any of my business," Kate commented.

Kate hadn't been there five minutes and she was already finding fault with me. Growing up with her, I expected some kind of a remark about what I had chosen to do with my life.

I think we all were hoping that Jim would speak up, and we just sat there, waiting for him to have the chance to do so.

"Kim, I see that you have lost a little weight since high school. Not that you were fat or anything," Kate said.

All I could think about was *here we go again* with the big sister who was always slender, tall and gorgeous. Who knew, she might accidentally eat something today!

"Oh yes, I was a little overweight back then, Kate, and you forgot short too, but just so you know, I can drive that bad boy rig of mine that is parked in the drive to the moon and back!" I replied, feeling disgusted with her.

At that time, Aunt Betty asked me to help her get some crackers to go with the tea, and I knew what she was doing, but went with her anyway. Still feeling somewhat hurt by Kate, my next thought was maybe she should have taken a class called "How to Keep Your Mouth Shut."

"Kim, dear, I know that you and Kate haven't been that close growing up, or even now, like you and Ellen are. After all, she is quite a bit older than you are. I know that she really didn't mean to hurt your feelings. Over the years, she has grown in her modeling career and sometimes, like when she was young and still in school, forgets to 'zip her lips.' "

With that being said, I felt better and laughed out loud at Aunt Betty's words of wisdom. She was the one person who could always see a silver lining at the end of a rainbow, even when all I saw were clouds.

When I sat down in a chair close to the sofa, Jim looked at me and said, "Thank you, Kim, for not smacking Kate up alongside the face earlier, when she was being rude to you. I know, for a fact, that she really does love you," Jim commented.

"Thank you, Jim. How have you been, and are you still the CEO of that magazine company?"

"Yes, I have been doing this for many years, and like you loving your job, I love mine as well."

The rest of the day went all right. Kate managed to let Jim talk some, and everyone else too. It wasn't long after dinner when Allen and his family left to go to a hotel, where they had chosen to stay for the night. Kate and Jim retired to the bedroom across from the one that I was staying in, and it was time for me to enjoy some alone time in Aunt Betty's kitchen at the table. I had fixed some coffee and thought that I could unwind some before going to bed.

To my surprise, Kate also had the same idea and came in to sit and drink coffee with me.

"I'm surprised to see you still up, Kim," Kate said.

"I enjoy winding down sometimes, and at night is the perfect time for me to do this."

"I know what you mean, Kim. There are days when I do this at home as well. With my job, I am on my feet a lot and around many people all day. Don't get me wrong as I, like you, love my job. There are times when I get sent to Europe to model, and am gone for days at a time. Jim is very good about understanding this. At night, when he goes to bed, I enjoy alone time to find my inner peace.

"Just so you know, Kim, I am sorry for what I said to you today. I was really out of line talking to you like that. I know that you are doing something with your life that you really want to do, and I am proud of you for that. You are, most of the time, your own boss, and have the time it takes to be alone and enjoy traveling and seeing things that you have never seen before, and you don't have someone looking over your shoulder, telling you what to do, or where you made a mistake. I really do envy you for that. At times. I have been known to say the wrong thing, and today was the prime example of it. The one thing that I always want you to remember is that I love you and want you to be safe," Kate said with a tiny tear dropping from her left eye.

"I know, Kate, as I have always looked up to you. What you have chosen to do with your life is admirable, and I know time-consuming. I know growing up, we weren't the closest of siblings, and that is because you and Allen are so much older than I am. I would like it if we could find a way to start over, moving forward, and see each other more than we have, and not just here at Aunt Betty's home," I replied.

"Kim, I would love that. Maybe you can come to New York and I can show you around. If you want, you can also watch me model. I don't want it to be that years from now we are regretting not spending more time together," Kate commented.

"I agree, and I will find the time to visit you in New York. It is late and I need to sleep. I can't wait to see the big surprise that Ellen has for us tomorrow."

"Me too, Kim. She was always full of surprises," Kate said with a chuckle.

After way too many years, Kate and I finally had a chance to connect. I was sure that I knew more about why she behaved the way she did. Now, instead of just remembering the way Kate and I were before, we could start over and make new memories that we would both remember from now going forward. Somehow or some way, maybe this was a ploy from Aunt Betty, throwing Kate and I together to work out our differences. I believe this talk was meant to happen.

—3—

TRUE OR NOT TRUE

When morning came, Allen had arrived early with his family, and Kate and Jim were already up, awaiting Ellen's arrival. Aunt Betty had made breakfast and had saved me some.

"Good morning. I must have really been tired to have slept this long. Has there been any word from Ellen?" I asked.

"No, not yet, and we are starting to get worried. If she isn't here by tonight, Marie and the kids and I are going to need to leave to go back home early tomorrow morning as I have work to do on location. We will just find out what her surprise is later. Hopefully, we can catch up with her another time," said Allen.

"The same goes for Jim and me, Kim. I have a modeling job late tomorrow afternoon, and we have our return flight scheduled for early in the morning. I hope everything is okay with her!"

"It's not like Ellen to say she will be here, and then not show up," Aunt Betty remarked.

"I still have plenty of time before my new haul, and so if she isn't here by tomorrow morning, I will go looking for her. Has anyone tried calling her today?" I asked.

"Yes, many times, and her phone just goes to her answering machine. We thought at first that maybe her phone wasn't working because of where she was on the highway, but now we aren't so sure," Aunt Betty commented.

"For now, let's just relax and wait to see what happens. I am sure that she is all right, or one of us would have heard by now," Marie remarked, trying to keep Aunt Betty calm.

So we agreed that Marie was right and that we just needed to sit and wait it out. I was pretty sure that whatever was happening, Ellen was fine and would have a good excuse why she got delayed. If nothing else, tomorrow morning I would take my tractor rig and go looking for her along the route that I knew she takes when she goes from her home to Aunt Betty's.

As the day progressed, everyone found themselves looking at their watches once in a while, to check the time. Aunt Betty was trying to be a good hostess and keep us entertained the best she could. In fact, Allen had sneaked off to the bedroom and called all the hospitals between here and Montgomery, Alabama, where Ellen lives. It was 160 miles from here and about a three-hour drive. This wouldn't take me long at all if I did need to find her.

Finally, it was time for dinner and still no phone call. As usual, the meal that Aunt Betty had fixed was wonderful, but it seemed as if none of us had much of an appetite. I helped her clear the table and Kate did the dishes.

Later that evening, Allen and his family left for the hotel, informing us that if we heard from Ellen, to let him know right away. I told him I would, and they said their goodbyes before leaving.

After Jim and Aunt Betty went to bed, Kate and I stayed up awhile, talking. Around 11:00 p.m. she announced that she had to go to sleep. I agreed as I told her that it looked like I was needed to find Ellen and was very much in need of getting some rest before I left the house.

Night time went fast, and still no word from Ellen. Now we were all very worried. Aunt Betty called the hospitals like Allen had, and notified the police and the state patrol to be on the lookout for her as she was becoming a missing person. As old as she was, it worried me as I didn't want her having health issues from overloading her mind about Ellen.

Soon after Kate and Jim told us both goodbye and to call them the minute that I found her, or if she turned up after they left, I assured them, just like I did Allen and Marie, that I would find her, no matter where she had gone to or was at.

At that time I told Aunt Betty that I would be back with Ellen, but that I wasn't sure when. This could take me more than one day, I explained, and that if possible, I would keep in touch with her and she was not to worry about either one of us. I hugged her goodbye and walked out the front door to my rig, to start it and leave once again on my journey.

I knew the route so well that this would be the easy part of the search. The rest of it was going to be much harder. I had a recent picture of her that was in my wallet. I also knew the places where she might stop and eat, get gas, or rest. This, through our conversations on the phone in the past, had given me information that would be very helpful now.

As I drove, I not only watched the highway, but also looked at everything else, hoping to see Ellen's car. My first stop was going to be at a gas station that she went to each time that she visited Aunt Betty.

The place was practically empty as it was a Sunday, and my guess was that most of the customers had already gone to church. I didn't see Ellen's car anywhere as I drove to this place, and it wasn't sitting there, but I would ask some questions while I was there.

"Good morning," I said to the clerk.

"Good morning to you as well, young lady," he replied. "Can I help you find something in here?" he asked.

"No, not this time, but I do have a question for you, and I am hoping that the answer is yes."

"I will try to help you the best way that I can," he said.

"I have a picture of my sister Ellen, and would like you to look at it. She was supposed to be at our aunt's house in Atlanta a couple of days ago, and she never showed up."

"Sure, I'll take a look at her picture. Maybe she changed her mind and decided not to go to your aunt's house after all," he replied.

"When we spoke to her last, she was on her way and said that she was excited to see all of us, so I think that she would have let us know if she had changed her mind," I replied.

I then pulled out my wallet and showed him her picture.

"Oh yes, I know Ellen. She is a regular customer of ours from time to time, when she is passing through here. She always has a smile on her face and has always been very well liked by all of us who work here," he commented.

"Did you see her within the last couple of days?" I asked.

"I didn't, but maybe a co-worker of mine did as she doesn't always stop here when I am working. When she comes to work, I will find out for you if she has seen her, and if you will give me your phone number, I will give you a call later on today and let you know if Ellen stopped here and around what time."

"Yes, I will, and that would be very helpful. Meanwhile, this will give me a chance to check other places where she has been known to go. Thank you for your time," I said as I was leaving the building. I had given the man my phone number and now would be waiting for his phone call. Time would tell if she had made it that far. Then, at least, I would have an idea where to look next.

It was not like her to not call if she had decided to go back home. Even though I was trying not to think the worst, it was too late as it was already implanted inside me.

Down the highway was a restaurant with a huge parking lot, so I knew that I could park my tractor rig there without causing other people to need to drive around the block, looking for a place to park. I was hungry and suffering from deprivation from all the questions and worry of wondering where Ellen was. Would this be the restaurant where she ate this time?

When I walked through the door, a lady showed me to a table. She was wearing a pin that told me her name and that she was the manager. This might be helpful as I knew that a manager works longer hours and more shifts than just a person who works for six or eight hours and then goes home. As she seated me, I asked her if she had the time to answer a question for me.

"I am sorry to bother you as I am sure you are very busy, but I need to find my sister, Ellen. She has been missing now for a couple of days, and my family and I are very worried about her. I have a picture of her and would like you to take a look at it and tell me whether you have seen her before," I said.

"Yes, I can do that for you. There are many places to eat out around here and she might have chosen a different one."

"My sister is quite traditional. She has been this way her entire life, but there is that possibility that she could have eaten elsewhere. Right now I am desperate to find her," I said as I pulled her picture from my wallet.

The lady manager looked hard at it and wanted to make sure she was certain before giving me an answer. "No, I haven't seen this woman in here at any time. That doesn't mean that she hasn't been here as I am the day manager and we also have a night manager. If you will give me your phone number, I will ask her and all of the employees if they have seen her," she replied back.

I showed her the photo of Ellen and she walked away, telling me that she would call me to let me know. The waitress came to take my order and I was getting frustrated. I felt like I was looking for a needle in a haystack. Ellen could be anywhere. This search could take weeks or even months, and I wanted to find her *now!* I was scheduled for a haul in a couple of weeks, and with this, knowing that I could only search for so long and then it would be up to the police and state patrol to find her.

Once again, the waitress repeated herself and I apologized to her for staring and not responding. I told her that I had to find my sister and also showed her Ellen's photo. She, like the manager, hadn't seen Ellen, so it was another huge disappointment for me. I ordered what I wanted to eat and left, taking it with me.

Again, I was on the highway driving toward Montgomery in hopes that I found Ellen before I got to her home. I had a really bad feeling about this. The hard part was that she was so excited to tell us about a surprise that she had for us. It would have been nice if she would have just, this time, gone ahead and told us the surprise before she left home, and maybe this would have given me a clue as to where she was right now.

As the day progressed, I had driven for many hours, looking in every direction and on streets, hoping to get a glimpse of her or her car. The daylight was fading and I was headed for a truck stop, where I could park and sleep for the night. I did get a call from the man at the gas station, and the manager of the restaurant, both telling me that no one that worked at their places had seen Ellen. Feeling discouraged, I closed my eyes and lay in bed until I finally dozed off from exhaustion, wondering where she could be.

In the morning, I was on my way again to places where I had been told Ellen had stopped at along the way to Atlanta. Not seeing her car anywhere really gave me a sick feeling in my stomach, letting me know that whatever this was, it was something serious and that, for the first time in Ellen's life, she was in trouble and needed help.

About halfway into my stops and talking to many other people, I got a call from Allen. He and Marie had decided to help, and Allen had taken a flight to Montgomery, to go directly to Ellen's home to check and see if she was there and okay. While there, he was going around talking to all of her neighbors and asking them when was the last time they had seen her.

Her next-door neighbor said that she had seen Ellen three days ago and, at that time, Ellen appeared to be in a big hurry. Marie had gone to stay with Aunt Betty, to try hard to keep her calm and help her with everything she could. Kate and Jim wanted to also be involved in the search for Ellen, but couldn't be as Kate had a photo shoot in Paris and was scheduled to be there for several days.

Everywhere I went it was the same news, except for a coffee shop in Lankford that Ellen had eaten in. The waitress knew her and said that she had seen her three days ago. They had talked and Ellen had been excited about seeing all of us.

This was what I had been waiting for as at least I knew that she had made it that far, and so I needed to backtrack from there and not just look in the towns but also take some side highways, in case she had changed her mind for some reason and decided to take a different route.

I thanked the waitress and called Allen to tell him what I knew. He told me that he had gotten some newspapers to look at, to see if maybe she might have been involved in a serious car accident, or worse. He had already called the morgues and hospitals. He also notified the police departments about her being a missing person. They told him that they would keep an eye out as well for her, and let the surrounding areas be aware of this.

Allen also told me that there had been a hold-up at a gas station and a bank between Montgomery and Atlanta, and he was wondering if maybe Ellen had seen it happen and was afraid and hiding somewhere. With him being a movie producer, his mind was helpful as he was thinking of things that my mind wouldn't have thought about. I told him that if Ellen was in danger and I did find her, I would dial her home phone and let it ring, but not give my name, but instead a code of numbers, being an address and town and also a street, if possible, of where we both were. This was the only way to keep us both safe. Allen then said that he would take it from there to help. I told him that worked and we both ended our call. I had come to an old highway, where I turned off. It looked pretty much deserted, and was one that I had never traveled on, not knowing where it came out.

I drove for an hour, and once again didn't see her car. I had decided that when I found her and all of this was over with, I would probably need another couple of weeks to recover and rest from this escapade that I have been on.

This highway was not one that Ellen had ever taken or told me about. So I knew that if I did find her car, she would be somewhere not far from it, or then again maybe she might be hitchhiking to Atlanta. My thoughts were all over the map and I had to stay calm myself, so I could have a clear mind.

Before I went any further, I pulled off the highway and called Allen. I had a hunch and wanted to see if it paid off.

"Hello, Kim. Did you find her?" Allen asked frantically.

"No, not yet, but you said something earlier that caught my interest. You had said that there was a hold-up at a gas station and a bank three days ago. What is the name of the gas station, and what town did it happen in?"

"The gas station is called Blair's. It is in Lankford," Allen replied.

"That makes sense as the waitress at the cafe told me that she had seen Ellen three days ago, and the cafe is in Lankford. Blair's in one of the gas stations that Ellen has talked about, and maybe the person who works there might know if she was there the day of the robbery. I will turn around and go back there and ask questions."

"Kim, if this looks like it is also going to put you in danger, I don't want you doing this. I can call the police department there and maybe they will be able to help instead of you," Allen commented.

"I will be fine, Allen. I am sure that the police are looking for the robbers right now as well, and maybe by tomorrow morning they might have captured them and also found Ellen. This is something, though, that I need to do to maybe lead me to her," I replied.

"Okay, Kim. If this is what you want to do, but be careful as neither one of us knows the mess that Ellen could be in right now."

"I will. Don't worry," I told him.

I turned my tractor rig around and headed back to

Lankford. It wouldn't take me long as I had just left that town about an hour ago. I might be wrong and Ellen might not have stopped there that day.

When I pulled into the gas station, I saw a car that looked like hers parked on the side of the building. I got out and walked over to it. I couldn't tell without entering it, and didn't want to do that before talking to the man who ran the place as I could be wrong about the car.

When I entered, I saw the man stocking some shelves and asked him if I could have a little bit of his time. He then told me yes, and so I showed him Ellen's photo. He told me that the last time he had seen her was three days ago, and it was the day that his gas station had been robbed.

I asked him about what time he had seen her, and he said just a few minutes before, three men had entered his place, carrying guns and demanding money from him. He told me that he found her car sitting on the side of the building and that he had been waiting for her to come back and get it. I told him I had been looking for her for days and that when I found her, she would get her car. He said that worked for him, and that he wouldn't have it towed off.

Before leaving the gas station, I asked him if the police had found the robbers and was told no, that they were looking for them all around town. He said that he was sure they weren't anywhere near town as they had gotten away with a large amount of money. Not just from the bank, but from his gas station as well.

He also mentioned the old highway outside of Lankford that I was on, and said that one of the men that robbed him looked like someone he had known when the man was young and used to come in there with his mother all the time to get gas. He said that if it was the same person, his parents might still have a cabin off the old highway and that he had told the police officer this on the day of the robbery. They told him that they would check out the cabin if they couldn't find the men in Lankford.

I thanked the older man and told him that he had been a

big help to me, and that we would be back to get her car. The man's story sounded good, and I knew that police officers don't look in just one town, in one area, and won't stop until they find who they are looking for, no matter what it takes.

Either this man was wrong about the robber, or maybe the law enforcement had found all of them and Ellen wasn't with them.

After I walked out of the gas station, I went to her car. It was unlocked, and so I began searching desperately for a clue that might lead me to her. I rubbed the seats with my hand, looking for anything and everything. Not just in the front seat, but also the back seat. Also the floor, and when I stuck my hand down between the console and the driver's seat, I found her cell phone. This was a clue that she had been taken away by force as Ellen takes her phone with her, no matter where she goes.

I opened it and checked out her dialed calls, to see who the last person was that she had spoken with. The number listed last was Aunt Betty's number. The same applied to received calls. There were some from Allen and myself. I took her phone and checked to see if she had left her key in the glove compartment. If so, this could indicate that she had put it there in hopes that someone would find her key and move the car before it got towed away. I was fishing for excuses, and there was no key.

Allen was still at Ellen's house and so I called him.

The phone rang a couple of times and then Allen answered. "Kim, any news?"

"I haven't found her yet, but I have found her car and her cell phone. It was stuck between the console and the driver's seat. Her car was unlocked and there's no spare key in the glove compartment or the console. The man at the gas station did tell me that she had been there just a few minutes before the robbers, who robbed the bank and his place, robbing him of a bunch of money. He told me that he wouldn't have her car towed, and I told him we would pick it up as soon as I found her.

"The older man seems to think that one of the men is a grown man now that used to come there with his mother when he was younger. He also mentioned a cabin that the grown man had lived in with his family. He told me that it is on that same old highway that I had turned off on. I drove down it for a while before I talked to you, and came back here. Now I am not sure what to do as Ellen could be anywhere," I said.

"Kim, you have done a bunch! All of this sounds to me like she was taken from her car against her will. Maybe the men were the ones that did this, or maybe she got scared and left her car to run someplace else. In the excitement, she may have forgotten to grab her phone. If she did do this, by now she would have gone back. I am assuming he told the officer about this."

"Yes, he did, and I know that they put everything that he told them in their report. By now I would have thought that they would have found the men and also Ellen, if they took her," I commented.

"Right now they might be trying to find the cabin that the man is talking about, or it may no longer exist. Maybe it was torn down at one point, and the man didn't know about this. I am just glad that he didn't have her car hauled away."

"Me too, and the only way to know if the cabin is still standing is to go back to the highway and drive until I either see it, or keep going until I run out of it. If I do find it, I will check to see if it is empty. No matter what, I will call you and keep you updated," I replied.

"Okay, Kim, but you need to remember that these men are dangerous and I can't imagine the three men staying there for very long. If it is true that one of the robbers suspects that the gas station owner recognized him, they might be long gone by now. Just be careful, Kim. Don't get put in an awkward situation," Allen said.

"I will do my best not to."

It was the end of our conversation, and once again time for me to find a spot to park for the night. I would drive down the old highway again in the morning to wherever ... and hopefully find Ellen.

As I was driving to the gas station, I noticed a small public park with areas where anyone who had a camper or RV could park for the night. This would be where I ended my day.

—4—

SEARCH AND SITUATION

The next morning, feeling exhausted still, even after dozing on and off all night with many things going through my mind keeping me awake more than not, I needed coffee. Today when I was driving around, I would be not just watching the highway in front of me, but looking at everything surrounding me. The sun hadn't been up long, and I was getting an early start. Time was of the essence now as, if it was true and the three men were holding Ellen hostage, and with the danger she might be in, I would find the strength and courage to continue on.

Driving slowly, I was an hour into the search. The only building I had seen was an old run-down warehouse. There were a few cars parked in front of it. As the day progressed, I had driven many miles. I finally came to a connecting highway with lots of traffic and no highway to continue onto if I crossed that one. The old highway had run out.

My search for Ellen was leading me nowhere and I was feeling overwhelmed, not knowing what to do next. So far, I had been going on assumptions and with the only hunch left inside me, I had to go with it, not knowing whether it would turn out to be anything.

I turned my tractor around and started back the way I had come. Once again, I looked in every direction along the highway, trying to find this cabin that the man spoke about. There was no cabin. Just the warehouse and no connecting road going east or west off of the old highway. The only thing running alongside it was miles of fence line. Maybe Allen was right and the cabin had been torn down. Maybe someone had bought the cabin and built a warehouse beside it, or just torn down the cabin, leaving the warehouse. This was turning into a mind twister and my mind was running in circles. This was not good as I needed a clear one as Ellen's life depended on it.

The only way to know whether any of what I had thought about was true meant that I would need to stop at the warehouse and walk up to it, and look through the windows, unless someone was outside in the yard. If that didn't work out the way I planned it, there would be nothing left to do but walk up to the front door and knock.

What I should have done was called Allen, to let him know what I was about to do. But instead, I continued to drive back the way I had just come. When I did get close to the warehouse, I would park my tractor rig off the highway, a ways away from the warehouse, where it couldn't be seen. In my mind I was planning a sneak attack.

As I was walking up to it, I could hear talking. If I was right and Ellen was in there, she wouldn't be the only one with a surprise. Being short didn't help as some of the windows were too high up for me to look through, and there was nothing in sight for me to stand on to give me the height I needed.

I had walked softly around the building and no one was in the yard. Wondering whether I should stay there or go back to the truck and call Allen on an assumption that might turn out to be nothing, as Ellen might not be there. I also didn't know if the police would storm the warehouse with maybe nice people in there, making Allen's credibility and mine look bad, and then no one would help me.

Neither Allen nor I needed this, so I decided that there was only one thing to do, and that was to just walk up to the front door and knock. This might not be the smart thing to do, but without knowing, it was the only thing that I could do. If this turned out badly, I would need to figure out how to make things good again for Ellen and for myself.

Standing at the door with my hand up, ready to knock, I saw it open. Standing there was a tall older man who, at the moment, looked as surprised as I did. There was no turning back now as I had been seen and had to come up with a really good story on why I was there.

"Hello. My car broke down about a mile from here. Is it all right if I come in to use your phone to call for a tow truck?" I asked.

"Sure, you can come in, young lady," the man replied.

The look in his eyes had me worried then as now I was wondering if he was a robber or something else and liked young women.

"Thank you," I replied.

When I entered the building, I expected to see all kinds of tools and an automotive shop of some sort. Instead, what I saw were many rooms and an actual house.

Standing in the room with us was another man, and then another man came from a different room. One of the other men was also tall and older as well, like the one that had answered the door. The younger man came from the bedroom. Was this man the one that the owner of the gas station had referred to?

The two older men looked at each other funny, and then when I asked again to use the phone, the man who answered the door grabbed me and hung onto me as I kicked and screamed. I was scared out of my mind, not knowing what they were going to do with me. Again, weighing 110 pounds and being 5-foot-2 never turns out good in a bad situation.

While one man held me and my arms behind my back, the other, older man tied a rope firmly around my wrists.

"We are not sure how you knew to come here, lady, but you look a lot like another guest that we have here. You should have stayed away!"

I tried telling them that it was true and that I needed help from a tow truck, but neither one of the older men believed me. The younger man stood there and said nothing. They took me to a semi-dark room and threw me into it, locking the door behind me. When I turned around, lying on the floor was my sister, Ellen. She looked very tired, but she wasn't hurt in any way.

"Kim, you shouldn't have come looking for me!"

"What are little sisters for, if they can't get themselves in a mess like their older sister?" I replied with a smile as I had finally found her.

"How did you know where to look?" Ellen asked.

"Through what Allen had discovered and a few hunches that paid off. We have been looking for you for days," I replied.

"So does Allen know where we are?"

"Not exactly, but he knows about where I was going to look for you. Hopefully, if I can't, he will figure out a way to get us out of here." Then I asked, "How did you end up here, Ellen?"

"I ate at a café that I have told you about and then stopped at Blair's gas station to get gas. I paid the owner, and as I was walking out, I walked past these men that are here. Not thinking anything about it, and them being robbers, I went back in to get some coffee to take with me as I drove. When I opened the front door before I walked in, I saw them standing there holding a gun on the man. The money was already in a paper bag and they were getting ready to leave.

"They saw me, and when I shut the door to run away, they caught me and dragged me to their car with one of the men having his hand over my mouth so that I couldn't scream. They threw me in the back seat and one of the men sat there watching me, holding his gun on me so that I wouldn't try to escape or jump out. They brought me here, tied my hands up with a rope, and put me in here just like they did you."

"I found your car at Blair's as Allen told me the name of the gas station that was robbed, and I remembered the name as one that you had told me about, where you got gas in Lankford. I had already spoken with a waitress at the café, and she had told me that you ate there and how excited you were to be going to Atlanta to spend time with your family. Allen had read about the three men in the newspaper and told me about them.

"When I found your car and spoke to the owner, Allen and I were pretty sure that you were being held hostage. He is staying at your home and has been for a few days now. We have been working together to try to find you. So now that I am with you, Ellen, what is the surprise that you have for all of us?" I asked.

"I am pregnant, Kim. I have been for three months now. My boyfriend, Scott, is stationed at Fort Belvoir, Virginia. He only has a year left in the military, and then he will be able to retire. We connected almost the moment we saw each other. I wanted to tell you and the rest of the family before I told him. Now I might not get the chance. Where these men have guns, I don't know if they are killers. We have to find a way out of here, Kim. We just have to!" Ellen said with tears streaming down her face.

"Don't worry, Ellen, I won't let anything happen to you or the baby. Just stay calm and some way we will be okay. As long as we both do what they tell us to do, I don't think they will hurt us. Eventually, Allen is going to start to wonder why I didn't call him back, and he'll start worrying about not just you, but me as well. He will find a way to get us out of this mess if I can't.

"There is nothing that would have kept me from coming to look for you. Marie is with Aunt Betty, to keep her calm, and Kate wanted to come and help find you, but she got stuck needing to be in Paris for a photo shoot. All I want you to do is just lie there and rest," I said, hoping that what I had told her about making it out of here alive was what would happen. Also about Allen finding us in time.

The news that Ellen had for all of us was nothing that I expected it to be. If I couldn't come up with anything to get us safe and out of this mess, all I could do was hope that Allen didn't wait too long to seek help for us, and also that he didn't come storming in here himself or he would be in the same mess that Ellen and I were in. I guess this is kind of what they mean when they tell people not to take the law into their own hands. Again I should have listened to Allen and just talked to the officers in hopes of them helping us find Ellen.

The way that the three men had the bars on the window made it difficult to know if it was still day or night time. My inner feeling told me that it was night time as I didn't hear anyone talking in the other room, and I was tired. Now that I had found Ellen, I knew I could sleep, but it was going to be on the floor with our wrists tied.

Sometime during the night when I was sleeping, I was awakened by the men talking. Their conversation wasn't as clear as I would have liked it to be, but I did pick up on most of their words.

"Ben, I haven't said anything before now, but it is time to say something."

"What do you have to say, Jerry? Whatever it is, make it fast as I have some work to do tonight on the car, to get it ready to leave here," Ben replied.

"If that other woman could find us, then don't you think more people will come looking for them, and us?" Jerry asked.

"Jerry, I think you are just letting your imagination get the best of you. How that woman found us was a long shot. If anyone else was going to find us, it would have happened before now. The cops don't have a clue where we are at. All you need to do is just be patient as we will be out of here in a couple of days," Ben said.

"Where is Kaylob? He left early to go get us some grub. He should have been back by now," Jerry said.

"I'm not sure, but I do know that you are worrying way too much. That is what will get us in trouble, if you don't stop!" Ben told Jerry with a disgusted look on his face.

"All right, Ben, I will try to stay calm, but I don't have a good feeling about this. When I agreed to be a part in the holdups, I only did it so that my sister would have money to raise her baby when it is born. You told me that this would be a smooth operation, and that I wouldn't need to worry about anything going bad as it was cut and dry," Jerry commented.

At that time I heard the front door slam and it was once again quiet in the house. I assumed that the man called Ben had gone outside and the other man called Jerry probably was pacing the floor, waiting for the third man called Kaylob to get back. I wasn't sure, but I felt like Jerry was scared of getting caught by the police and that he might be the one I could trick into helping us escape. He said that he had done this for his sister because she was pregnant, just like Ellen. Hopefully, I could play with his emotions. Now that I had heard his voice, if he came in here I would know which one of the three men I was talking to. I had already heard Ben's voice at the door.

Before I went back to sleep, I looked at Ellen, sleeping peacefully on the floor next to me, and could see that she was sleeping very soundly. When I found her, I had seen how weak she was from lack of food and water. All I could think about was how I could get her some as she and the baby needed it.

It had been a day since I had spoken to Allen. I knew that he was now not only worried about Ellen, but also about me. By now I was sure that he had called my cell phone a dozen times, hoping that I would pick up and answer it. He knew the route that I was taking as I had told him that I was going to check out the old highway once more. The only thing that could stop him from knowing exactly where we were was that he would be looking for a cabin like I was. All I could do was sit here and pray that he figured it out like I did, and would go to the police with information, and that they would take it seriously and come out here and find us. We were running out of time, and before long there would be no hope for Ellen or me.

During the night I had seen the door open and the older

man that had come in here was shining a flashlight around in the room, to make sure that we weren't doing anything that he didn't like. I lay still like Ellen, and pretended that I was sleeping. Apparently these men were crazy and I had to keep Ellen safe. She was carrying a tiny gift that would give all of us joy and happiness.

Later, I listened and once again overheard a conversation between the men named Kaylob and Ben.

"What took you so long last night getting back here?" Ben asked.

"I had to drive to Delta Junction to get our grub. Our faces are plastered all over the newspapers and fliers that have been placed all around town. I couldn't run the risk of me being identified by anyone. I will be glad when you have that car fixed so that we can get out of the area," Kaylob remarked.

"If everything continues to go good, I will have it fixed in a couple of days. We would use one of the other cars if they weren't used in the robbery of the bank and gas station. We would be spotted in a second. Just remember this when you are driving again, if I need you to. You have been taking a risk going into town, and this time you did the right thing by driving to another place," Ben replied with a sober face.

"Ben, I noticed a tractor rig last night a piece down the highway, and it looked empty, but then again I thought that maybe someone might be sleeping in it and had pulled off the highway for the night. I didn't check it out inside," Kaylob said.

"You know that this is nothing unusual as there are many truckers that use this old highway to get to the other connecting highway. They have been doing this for many years. The tractor rig might have been broke down as well and the trucker might have had to walk until someone picked him up to give him a ride. I am sure that is probably what happened. I swear, Kaylob, you and Jerry are so skittish that you are making me that way, and I won't ever get that car fixed," Ben commented with disgust in his voice.

Kaylob had noticed my tractor rig. Because he and Ben, like so many other people, think that only a man is the trucker behind the wheel of a tractor, it normally would upset me. But today I was very grateful for this, for if they knew that I was the trucker, they might drive my rig away from here and no one would ever find Ellen and me when the three men left us alive.

As bossy as Ben was, I could tell that he was the leader. He was good at giving out orders, and Kaylob and Jerry were good at following them. Whether they were brothers or just friends, I didn't know, but I did know that they had made some bad choices. They can run, but they won't ever be able to hide, as eventually they will get caught.

Ellen had opened her eyes and managed to sit up like I did. I could see that if I didn't find a way to get her some food and water, there would be a good chance that she and the baby would be in serious trouble.

"Good morning, Kim," Ellen said.

"Good morning. Do you feel okay?" I asked.

"I am very weak, Kim. It has been many days since I last had anything to drink or eat. I am more worried about my baby than myself," Ellen commented.

"I am going to try to fix this today for you. No matter what I say, I need you to go along with it," I replied.

"Okay, Kim. Just be careful as these men appear to be dangerous."

"Last night I was able to listen to some of their conversations and also this morning. One of the men is named Jerry. From the sound of his voice, he appears to be the youngest of the three men. He also is very nervous since I arrived here, thinking that there will be more people who will start snooping around. He is worried that they are going to get caught.

"I am pretty sure that the oldest man, Ben, is the leader as he has been directing orders to both of the other men, and they are following whatever he says. Ben seems like he is a hard-hearted man. Kaylob, the second oldest man, left last night to go to another town to get them food. The police have fliers with their names and pictures all over town, and also in the newspapers.

"So Kaylob went to a different town as he was afraid of being identified. He appears to be somewhat skittish. He managed to see my rig sitting off the highway and assumed that the man driving it might be asleep, so he didn't go check it out. Ben told him that the man who drove the truck could have been hitchhiking as well, because it might have broken down. He also told Kaylob that he is way too skittish, like Jerry, and if they didn't stop, he would also become that way and never get the car fixed that they are planning on leaving in.

"For once in my life, I am so happy that they think a man is the trucker and not me."

"I'm happy they don't know that you are the driver, Kim. Hopefully, Allen will send out someone to look for your rig, and when they see it, they will come here to see if you are in here, and then we both will be safe again," Ellen replied.

Ellen, feeling weak, lay back down on the floor to rest. As I sat there, the youngest man came into the room with the flashlight, shining it around. This was the opportunity I had been waiting for as I needed to play on Jerry's emotions, if I could.

"Excuse me, can I talk to you for a minute?" I asked.

"Yes, I suppose so, but make it quick," Jerry replied.

As soon as I heard his voice, I knew it was the man named Jerry and the only hope that we had left.

"Thank you for your time. I just found out that this woman is pregnant. I think there was a misunderstanding with assuming that we are related. It is just a coincidence that we look similar. Because she is carrying a child, she needs food and water. She told me that she hasn't eaten in many days. I am asking you if you will bring her some. I don't need anything for myself, but if you can, please help her," I said.

"I am sorry to hear this. Even if I wanted to do this, I don't know if I could. The old man is very firm on what he is telling us to do. If I do get the chance without the others seeing me, I will bring what I can to her. My sister is also going to have a baby before long, and I wouldn't want her to do without food and water. I will see what I can do for now," Jerry replied.

I could tell at that moment that Jerry did have a heart, so this confirmed that he might be our ticket out of here.

When the door shut to our room and he went back into the other one, I overheard Ben talking to him.

"What took you so long in there, Jerry?" Ben asked.

"I just wanted to check out the room and make sure that nothing had been tampered with. I know that their wrists are tied, but I didn't want to take a chance anyway," Jerry said.

"That is a good answer, Jerry. I would hate the thought of you betraying us. It wouldn't turn out good for you," Ben said as he gave Jerry a smirky smile.

"Oh, you don't need to worry about that, Ben. I have a pregnant sister to take care of," Jerry replied.

I could see that Jerry wasn't a bad person and that he probably just robbed the bank and gas station because of his sister needing money. With Ben questioning him, though, this could make it harder for him to be able to help Ellen. From what Ben had told him, there was a huge chance that if he even suspected Jerry of helping either one of us, he would shoot and kill Jerry, just like I was afraid that he was going to do to Ellen and me.

—5—

BIG BROTHER TO THE RESCUE

Meanwhile, as Allen sat at Ellen's home, he was frantic! He had called my phone many times and there was no answer. He was not sure if I had decided to take a different route than the one I had spoken to him about, so he continued to wait for a call from me. His mind was going in circles, and he finally called Aunt Betty's home to speak to Marie.

The phone rang twice and she answered.

"Hello, Allen?" Marie asked.

"Yes, it is me. Have you heard anything from Kim or Ellen?"

"No, Allen. When did you hear from Kim last?"

"I heard from her night before last. She was supposed to keep me updated on where she is and if she found a cabin where three men are holding Ellen hostage. At least this is what Kim and I think is happening. I am sitting here not knowing what I should do next as Kim could be anywhere, just like Ellen. Without substantial evidence, I am not sure if the police department in Lankford will help me find them. I have no solid information to give them on where Kim might be right now," Allen said.

"I was afraid of this, Allen. I wish I knew what to tell you to do, but I don't know what to say, other than Kim has been known to make decisions on her own and as much as she loves Ellen, she would put her own life on the line for her. As for our conversation, I will make up something to tell

Aunt Betty on who called as she has been a nervous wreck. At her age, this is not good, and I don't want her frightened any more than she is," Marie commented.

"I understand and I am going to give it a very short time, and then I am going to call the police or go see if they will help me find them. I know that they are in danger."

"All right, Allen. Just be careful as this might be the only chance that you have to help both of them. It sounds to me, like it does to you, that Kim has gotten in the same mess as Ellen has, and right choices now are needed as their time could be short," Marie spoke with worry in her voice.

My mind was also focused on Allen and I wondered if he had gone to the Lankford Police Department, trying to help us, or if he had a panic attack and was in a hospital somewhere.

Within a few hours I heard the front door shut. It had been fairly quiet in the house and this made me nervous. Did Ben get the car fixed earlier than planned and they left here, or was he just going outside to work on it again? Within minutes I saw the door to our room open again. I also saw the flashlight being shined around inside. Luckily it was Jerry, and he had brought a big plate of beans and a glass of water for Ellen.

He softly shut the door to the room and came over to us.

"Thank you for doing this for her," I said.

"I will be back in about twenty minutes to get the plate and glass. Make sure she eats as this is going to need to be quick. This is all the time that I have to spare," Jerry replied.

Giving it one more shot at his emotions, I said, "Thank you, Jerry, for doing this. I don't know what your reason is for doing what you did, but by doing this, I can tell that you aren't a bad person. Sometimes we all struggle and make wrong choices. From what you have said, I know that you would never want your sister's baby to die because of lack of food and water. I will make sure that this woman eats and drinks the water. Thank you again for doing this for her," I said with a smile.

I woke up Ellen and informed her that she had a plate of food to eat and water to drink. She turned over on her stomach and ate the food like an animal would, and then knocked the glass over into the plate, licking it up as a dog would have. When she was done, she wiped her mouth on my shirt so that the food didn't show on it, in case one of the other men came in here later to check on us.

When Jerry returned to get the plate and glass, I had one more shot at talking to him and I was going to take it.

"Thank you again for helping her. With you doing this, you might have helped to save the baby's life and this woman's. From you doing this, I can see that you aren't a killer. We both have families, just like you do, and need to go home. I am asking you to help us escape before you leave here. I don't know if the others have plans to hurt us or not, but like your sister who is carrying a baby, this woman wants to be around to hold her baby and watch it grow up," I said, trying to get through to Jerry.

"I know what you are saying, and I hear every word that you are speaking. The others haven't told me what they are planning to do with you two before we leave here. I will do whatever I can to save both of you from getting hurt or killed. I might have robbed a bank and helped hold up a gas station, but I am not a killer. I have my reasons for doing this as my sister needs help. I can't promise you that the others aren't killers. Before we leave, and if I can, I will bring this woman more food and water. That is the best that I can do. I have no control over what the other two choose to do before we leave," Jerry replied.

"Thank you for whatever you can do to help us," I said.

I had given it everything that I had inside of me, and I still believed that Jerry was a good person who had chosen a bad path to go on, in order to help his sister. Now all Ellen and I could do was sit here and wait to see if the police would rescue us first.

At Ellen's home, Allen had waited long enough. he had grabbed his bag and was on his way to Lankford to go to the gas station and talk to the owner. He had questions and needed answers to where exactly the old highway was. This was the only thing he knew of to do.

In the other room, again I overheard the conversation that was taking place.

"By tomorrow night I should be all done with the car. We will take care of business here and then be on our way. When we get to Tennessee, we will split the money and go our separate ways. The law will be looking for all three of us, and separately we stand a better chance of escaping," Ben said.

"Besides turning out the lights, grabbing our stuff and locking the door behind us, what do you mean by business, Ben?" Jerry asked.

"You don't think that we are going to walk out of here and let those women live, do you, Jerry?" Ben replied.

"Why wouldn't we, Ben? We would have no use for them, and eventually they would starve to death in here anyway, without us hurting or killing them. All we need to do is just worry about ourselves and leave here. It would be weeks or months before anyone would find them. They would be dead by then," Jerry said, trying to get Ben to rethink what he wanted to do with us.

"It sounds to me, Jerry, like you are kind of sweet on one of them. What are you doing when you go in to check on them?" Kaylob said with a laugh.

"Don't be silly, Kaylob! What kind of a fool do you take me for? I just don't see the need to kill them as they are going to die anyway. Without food and water, they don't stand a chance of living, and with the door locked, they couldn't open it up to escape anyway with their wrists tied together," Jerry commented back to Kaylob with anger in his voice.

"Okay, boys, stop bickering. When the time comes, we will decide what we are going to do. For now, get some sleep, Jerry, as Kaylob is taking the first watch for the cops," Ben said.

After that it got quiet in that room, and I wasn't sure what to expect, but I hoped that Jerry had a chance to get us out of here before it was time for them to leave. I could see that Ellen couldn't survive much more than what she had endured for days, and the waiting game was already causing my anxiety to shoot through the roof as I knew it was Ellen's.

I tried to sleep, but couldn't. The only good thing that I could think about was that I knew that by now Allen was doing everything he could to save us. Jerry was also trying his best to help us, but as stubborn as Ben was, I was afraid that Kaylob and Ben would overpower Jerry and it would be two against one.

Allen had reached Lankford and talked to the man who owned the gas station. He had gotten the same story as I had, and when Allen walked out of the gas station, he knew that he needed daylight to continue on. He could go to the police department with everything he knew, and what I had told him about the cabin, but Allen knew that the law was going to want more proof before they spent tax dollars, sending men out on an assumption that might not be true.

With the cabin being torn down and the only thing on the highway being the warehouse, Allen might not think about mentioning the warehouse to the authorities. For a couple of days, I had been twisting my hands around, trying to loosen the rope that was tied around them. I slipped my hands out of them and then untied Ellen's hands, telling her to hide her rope, and if anyone came through the door, to pretend like they were still tied. She said she would.

When morning came, I heard all three of the men talking again in the other room, which appeared to be the main room for conversation for them.

"Kaylob, I ran into another problem, and I need you to go back to Delta Junction and get a part for me. I tried to make the one I have work, but it is the wrong size. We need to get this put on the car and be ready to leave here before it gets too dark tonight. Today, don't take so long. Just get what I need and then get back here before noon. Once I get the part, it won't take long to finish fixing the car. Then we will be closer to leaving here with the money and splitting it up between all three of us," Ben said.

"Gotcha, Ben. Yes, I will hurry today," Kaylob said.

Jerry said nothing, and Kaylob was on his way out the door. The next few hours were going to be critical in what happened to us.

In Lankford, Allen was sitting at the police station. He had told them everything and was waiting for a reply back from the chief of police. At that time, Allen was also told that they needed to check and see if the old cabin was still there as there was a good chance that it wasn't, and that they weren't going there if there was nothing to go to.

Allen was getting very frustrated and wasn't going to take the law into his own hands, but he needed to drive on the old highway himself, to see what he could see. He told them that he knew that time was running out for us and that he felt like he had to do something to help. He also told them that if he could find something stating where we were, he would call them.

He left there and drove toward the old highway. An hour before he would be passing by the warehouse on the highway, he had called Marie again to let her know where he was at, and what his plan was. It would be a couple more hours before he would reach the connecting highway if he drove slow, like I had.

As he drove he looked all around and had seen the warehouse, but kept on driving. As I had, all he saw was the long fence line on both sides of the highway. When he got to the connecting highway, instead of crossing it, he did the same thing I did and turned around to go back the way he came.

By then Kaylob was back from Delta Junction with the part, and Ben was ready to put the part on the car. After that, Ellen and I would be at someone's mercy as Ben hadn't told Jerry whether he was going to kill us or not.

While Allen was driving back toward the warehouse, he

remembered the tractor rig that he had passed on the highway. When he passed it, he wasn't thinking about it being my rig as he had passed a couple of rigs when he was driving, going west in his search for us.

Ben had told Kaylob and Jerry that he had about one more hour and to be ready to leave there.

Not knowing where Allen was, my nerves were out of control, still trying to keep Ellen calm and hoping that somehow Jerry could save us. In the other room, Jerry was trying to think of his own plan to help us as he didn't trust Ben or Kaylob, and knew that they would kill anyone.

When Allen had reached my rig, he went to it and opened the door. He climbed inside of it and found not just my cell phone but also Ellen's. When he opened them up, he saw the numbers and calls that we had both made and he knew right away that we were in the warehouse. He called the police and told them again everything, and they said that several officers would be coming in on a helicopter and would be landing in the field. They told him to stay put in my rig. They were going to sneak up on the warehouse, in order to try to keep Ellen and me safe, and do a quiet attack that the men inside wouldn't see coming.

When Ben went inside, he told Kaylob to go in the room and take care of the problem in there. Jerry told Ben that as long as he was alive, they weren't going to kill anyone. Jerry told them that one of the women was pregnant, just like his sister, and there was no reason to kill us.

I quietly told Ellen to get up off the floor and to follow me to the door, where we would hide against the wall. If anyone came in there, our plan was going to be that we would jump whoever and try to knock him to the floor. She agreed, and so this is what we did.

If Kaylob or Ben came through the door, we would be able to take care of one of the men, in hopes that Jerry could take care of the other one.

"Jerry, you are kidding, aren't you?" Ben asked.

"What is wrong with you, Ben? You got what you wanted

when we robbed the bank and the gas station. There is no need to take those women's lives. I won't stand here and let you do it," Jerry said.

"You forgot, Jerry, you are up against two of us, and there is only one of you. Who do you think is going to come out on top? It won't be you, and if you want to die like them, then that works for us as then we will have more money to split between us," Ben said.

"No, Ben. There will only be one of you left, because either you or Kaylob are going to need to shoot me as well, and whoever goes in there, I am going to shoot first," Jerry said.

"Ben, I didn't sign on for this to get shot! Maybe you should rethink this with shooting anyone. What happened to you, Jerry?" Kaylob asked.

"Maybe I realized that what I did was wrong, and that I have a pregnant sister who is going to need help raising her child. I am going to turn myself in to the police if I don't get killed first," Jerry replied.

"What did I tell you to do, Kaylob?" Ben said with anger in his voice.

"No, Ben, I am not going in there. If you want those two women dead, you are going to need to do it yourself!" Kaylob replied with a firm voice.

"Oh, for Pete's sake. I will shoot them myself for you two pansies! If Jerry draws his gun, shoot him. We need to leave here, and time is running out on nonsense!" Ben said.

The helicopter had landed in the field, and the police officers were walking toward the warehouse. It wouldn't be long and they would be knocking down the door.

When Ben opened the door to our room, Jerry pulled out his gun to kill Ben. With Kaylob being scared of getting shot himself, he fired at Jerry, hitting him in the chest. Jerry fell over and onto the floor. When Ben walked into the room, he found two angry women waiting for him on the other side of the door. The minute he entered the room, Ellen and I jumped him, knocking his gun to the floor. I picked it up and had it pointed at him. Kaylob didn't have a chance to run as the police officers had knocked down the door and were standing inside the warehouse.

When they saw us coming out of the room, holding a gun on Ben, one of the police officers remarked in a joking way that we didn't need them at all, and that Ellen and I had things under control. If he only knew how hard I had prayed for them to show up there, he wouldn't have said that.

Of course I handed him the gun and then went over to check on Jerry. He was shot and still alive. I explained to the officers that he had saved our lives and was willing to turn himself in as he wasn't a killer, and I told them how he had given Ellen food and water when she needed it.

Ben stood there like Kaylob, in handcuffs, telling Jerry that he better hope that he died as neither one of them would forget what he had done to them, and to be very afraid as when they got out of prison, they would be coming after him. The only thing that Jerry said was, "Whatever." Then he passed out from pain. He was taken to the hospital right away.

When Allen saw Ellen and me walk out the front door, he blew my horn twice. He knew that would make me smile. Then he climbed down out of the cab and ran to both of us, to hug us like he hadn't ever done. I told Allen that Ellen had a huge surprise that was going to knock his socks off, but that she needed to go to the hospital to get checked out first. He agreed and they took us both. I could hear Allen saying that he didn't like surprises, and to just tell him what it was, and Ellen and I just smiled at him.

A police officer drove Allen's car back to Lankford, and Allen drove my tractor rig. By rights he wasn't supposed to as he didn't have a trucker's license, but the officer said that he would take the fallout from it, if anything was mentioned because of it. Allen loved it so much that he said that he might change careers. This made me laugh. He had called Aunt Betty, Marie, Kate and Jim, and told them everything.

After a few days in the hospital, Ellen was released. I

drove her back to Aunt Betty's, where everyone was waiting for her and me. When we walked through the front door, everyone screamed and roared from excitement, and we both once again got lots of hugs.

Ellen was ready to tell the rest of the family her secret. When everyone heard the news, there was another roar of delight and excitement. Then Ellen told everyone about Scott and how he would be the next one to find out.

Aunt Betty threw a party for Ellen and me. The whole family was there, celebrating.

As for Jerry, he recovered from the gunshot wound. Ellen and I had given the police department a written statement on how, if Jerry hadn't helped us, that we wouldn't be here now. When he went to court for the two robberies, the judge, after reading our report, gave him a light sentence of six months in jail.

When he was serving his time, I went to see him and told him that Ellen and I would be forever grateful to him and that I was sorry for lying to him about not being related to her. Jerry said that he forgave me already and wanted to remain being our friend. I assured him that we would be friends for life.

When Ellen had gotten back to Montgomery, she called Scott and told him everything. He was overwhelmed with happiness and over the phone he asked Ellen if she would be his wife. Of course, the answer was yes. Within a couple of months we all got together at Aunt Betty's home to attend the beautiful wedding.

—6—

CONNECTING IN UNITY

The day of Ellen and Scott's wedding, Ellen was dressed in a white flowing gown with a long flowing veil. Marie, Kate and I wore beautiful bridesmaid dresses that were alike but different colors. These gorgeous dresses were designed by none other than Ellen.

Kayla was the flower girl, and Rob was the ring bearer. Allen gave Ellen away, and Jim escorted everyone to their seats.

When the ceremony was over, when Ellen turned around to throw the bouquet, of course everyone stepped back and I was the designated one to catch it. My family and the other single ladies there just smiled at me, and I knew what they were thinking.

Would they get their wish? Time would tell. Ellen had invited Jerry's sister to the wedding. We all had fun holding her new baby. Whereas since Jerry was given a light sentence, Ben and Kaylob were given several years in prison. Jerry had written a letter to Ellen and me, telling us that after he got out, he was going back to school to be none other than an over-the-road truck driver like me. How ironic is that!

Ellen and Scott went on a well deserved honeymoon, and within a year Scott retired from the Army with full honors. He was content to live in Montgomery with Ellen and their new baby boy. They had named him Samuel Allen Robins. Samuel was our dad's name. A perfect name for such a perfect baby.

I continued to drive my bad boy from one state to another. In fact, along the way at a truck stop, I ran into Jerry. He had completed school and was on his way to making money the honest way. He had a new and exciting life ahead of him. When I told Aunt Betty about how Jerry had turned his life around, she once again said to keep my ears on. Again I couldn't stop laughing at what she had said.

Allen and Marie went to visit Aunt Betty more than they had before, like Kate and Jim did. I did my best to see her as much as possible. Also, I went to New York for a week to see Kate work, and to see the sights of the city with Jim. Sitting and watching Kate walk down the runway, modeling, was something that I will never forget! I was so proud of her and her accomplishments.

When Allen's new movie came out, I went to watch it at a theater, where I had stopped to rest for the night. Allen, like Kate, had more than excelled in his career, alongside Ellen, who would always be the one I shared a near-death experience with. We continued to talk on the phone almost every day. Scott and her are very happy, and so much in love.

Little Sam was growing and I knew it wouldn't be long before I would be on my way once again to Montgomery to see them all.

When Sam turned three years old, Ellen and Scott got the chance to go to Washington, D.C., and they asked me if Sam could ride along with me in the passenger seat for a week. I was thrilled and honored.

He really was excited when I blew my horn a couple of times for him each day. At a rest stop where we would eat, it was amazing to see the faces of the people standing around outside. When I stepped out of the cab with a three-year-old in my arms, there were many looks and a lot of smiles.

With all of the excitement that my family and I had shared together, I was certain that our mother and father were watching us from Heaven and smiling. We had become a bigger family and closer than we ever were before.

As for me, I am still content riding alone in my rig from one state to the other, but who knows, someday I might find the perfect man like Aunt Betty said my Uncle Henry was, but until then, I will continue to follow my dream as an over-the-road lady truck driver.

DEPRIVATION

PART IV

THE TOWN THAT DIDN'T EXIST

—1—

1912 AND MOVING FORWARD

As I walked, I heard the sound of my footsteps walking down a long hall leading to my grandfather's study, where he spent many hours typing one of many books that he had written over the course of his lifetime. As I pressed the light switch on the wall, I saw that I had entered a large room

In the room I saw several bookcases filled with novels of famous authors, such as William Shakespeare, Jane Austen, Edgar Allan Poe, Charles Dickens and many others. I was sure that if this oak desk could talk, it, too, would have many stories of its own to tell. In the middle of the desk was his last novel. Sitting in his chair, I opened it and started reading.

The year listed in the beginning of his book was 1912. Many things happened that year. On the introduction page he had indicated that New Mexico became the 47th state as Arizona became the 48th state. The Girl and Boy Scouts were founded, the overseas railroad opened, and the first train arrived in the Key West. Alaska became a territory of the United States, the famous Wilbur Wright died of typhoid fever, the White Star liner, *Titanic,* departed from Southampton with 2,225 passengers and crew on it, bound for New York on April 10, and on April 14-15 it struck an iceberg in the Northern Atlantic and sunk, taking with it 1,517 lives. The wreck of the ship wasn't discovered until 1985. In November, Woodrow Wilson became the President.

Grandfather told about many other occurrences that happened that year. He wanted to take his readers back to the year when his story began.

As I sat in his chair, reading and turning pages, I read this. My name is Albert Weatherton. I grew up in the city of Philadelphia. It was 1912. Being a small lad of six, I would go to my father's place of business after school. He owned a meat store and was also a butcher.

One day after school, I was told by my teacher that my mother needed me to come straight home. That particular day I wouldn't be hanging out with Father until he hung his "closed" sign on the door.

When I arrived at our home, I saw five older women sitting on the sofa, sipping tea. All of them, including Mother, were wearing what every woman wore at that time—long dresses that reached the floor and large hats.

Sitting on a chair was a girl about my age. She had gone there that day with her mother and was listening to all the women talking about many things as they visited, while also nibbling on tiny crackers.

When I shut the front door, Mother noticed that I was home. She called me over to her. "Albert, I am happy that you did as you were told as I have something that I want you to do," Mother spoke.

"Yes, Mother. What is it that you want me to do?" I asked, wondering why I was needed there and not by my father.

"This young girl has no one to talk to. I would like you to keep her company while her mother enjoys conversation," said Mother.

"I will do my best to, Mother. I really don't know what to talk to her about," I said.

"Talk to her about your school and your friends," she commented.

"Okay, Mother," I replied as I went to sit next to the young girl.

As I sat there with my hands folded, looking at her, I wasn't sure how to start the conversation. Being a boy and her being a girl made it difficult at the time for me to do this, but I would try.

"Hello, my name is Albert. What is your name?" I asked.

"My name is Emma," she said.

"Do you go to a school around here?" I asked.

"My father, mother and I just moved here and I haven't started school yet," Emma replied.

"Where did you come from?" I asked, feeling bored and wanting to go to my room.

"We came from a city called Chicago. I have no friends. Would you be my friend, Albert?" she asked.

"Yes, I suppose I can be your friend. Do you know how to play marbles?" I asked.

"No, but if you want to, you can teach me," she said.

I told her that I would. I ran up the stairs to my room to get the marbles. This was something that I did like to do. After I showed her how to play, it wasn't long until she caught on to the game.

A few hours later, it was time for the ladies to take their umbrellas that had been placed on a stand by the front door, where we also placed our coats, and return to their own homes. Emma told me that she would see me at school. I told her that I would introduce her to my friends. She waved goodbye to me, and her mother took her hand to walk out the door.

It wasn't long after that when Father returned home. His day was done, and like me, he was ready to eat. Mother informed both of us that it would be a while, so Father picked up his newspaper to read and I continued to play with my marbles.

The following week, Emma started school. It didn't take her long to make her own friends. We did continue to see each other at times. Sometimes I would go to her home with

Mother and she would come back to mine. At times she was even allowed to go with me to Father's meat store, where she would wait for her mother or father to come and get her.

Years passed quickly and we had both turned 16. The ladies in the city still wore the long dresses, large hats, and carried umbrellas. Most of the men wore hats, white long-sleeved shirts, ties, vests and suits. Some of them even carried a cane, and when they saw a lady, they would tilt their hat to show respect or just to say hello.

Cars were becoming more of a thing to see on the roads and streets, opposed to 1912, when mainly the rich families were the only ones who could afford to buy them. Some people still walked, rode bicycles, or used a horse and buggy as a form of transportation.

I was spending more time with my father, learning the family business. In a year or two, I would be out of school and would need a job full time. Being a butcher was something that I didn't want to be when I left home and was on my own, but until I had learned a new trade, it would get me by.

Emma and I were becoming better friends and were dating. She had blossomed into a beautiful young lady, who also wore long dresses, a large hat, and carried an umbrella. Father had bought us a Ford Model T, and I was allowed to drive it to take Emma home, or wherever else I was given permission to go.

Philadelphia was growing at a fast pace, more and more each year. It was becoming crowded. One day, Father mentioned to Mother that maybe they should move to a different place to live, and then after a discussion, they decided they should continue to stay here as Father would need to sell his business and then start over again in a smaller town or city.

After graduation, I hung around Philadelphia for a few years. I had a decision to make. Either I stayed there and continued to work for Father, or I left and learned a new trade.

Emma and I had become more than friends. I knew that

when, or where, I went to start a new life that I would be going alone. After being there for a while, I would then send for her.

The next week I was ready to leave. I had told Mother and Father goodbye, and that I would write when I got where I was going. Emma told me that she would wait to hear from me and then she would join me. Everything was said and I was boarding a train going west.

When I climbed onto it, to my surprise I was the only passenger. I found a seat and watched out the small window as we left the train station. I was leaving the only home I had and was on my way to a new life.

The conductor told me that was the first stop and one of many, and whichever one to stop at next would be one that I had chosen for myself.

I stayed on this train for days, and with each stop I would look through the window. I would choose the perfect place, where at that time I would get off the train.

I was confused as to why I was the only passenger riding this train, which had stopped many times in different stations, and I had seen others getting onto different ones. Why not this one?

When the conductor walked past me, I told him that I had a question for him.

"I would like to know why I am the only passenger on this train," I said.

"When you look around, this is what you see. In your mind, you chose to ride this train. Soon you will be ready to get off at a station," he replied.

When he said this, according to him I would reach my new destination before long.

It seemed like I had been traveling for five days, and as the train slowly moved through a town to its next stop at a station, I watched out the window and was certain that this town was where I wanted to be. When the door opened and I was standing there, ready to leave this train, I saw an old man standing outside, ready to get on. I spoke to him, but he never spoke back. He just stood there with a look of sadness.

I stood outside for a few minutes, looking at the people walking up and down the street. I noticed that they were wearing clothes different than what I was wearing, and going about their day.

When I crossed the street, I saw a woman sitting on a bench and I asked her where I could find a place to sleep for the night. She told me that the only room available might be at a big house on a street called Carver. I asked the woman how to get there, and she gave me directions.

As I walked up the steps and into the house, a man was standing behind a counter. He asked me if he could help me and I told him that I was new in town and needed a room to rent. He said that he did have one available, and that it would be five cents a day to stay there. I gave him the money for a week and thanked him.

Walking there, I had noticed a place to eat. I put my bags in my room and went outside again to walk back the way I had come. When I saw the place, I went in and sat down at a table. A young woman wearing an apron came over to me.

"Can I help you, or get you anything to eat, or drink?" she asked.

"Yes, I would like some eggs, bacon, toast and hot coffee," I replied.

I sat there, watching out the window of this tiny diner, looking at the people who were passing by. I wasn't sure yet if this was the town where I should be, but I did notice that the town and the people appeared to be nice. I saw a newspaper sitting on the table next to me and picked it up to read about the town. But before I could read much, the woman returned with my food and coffee.

After I was finished, I walked back to my room to sleep. I knew that if I wanted Emma to be with me, I had to find a job soon.

The next morning I was walking around town again, looking at the buildings and asking everyone I saw if they knew of anyone who was hiring. I continued to get the same answer, which was no.

After many days of doing this, I decided that there was a reason why I was to get off of the train that I was riding, instead of continuing on, going further west.

A man had told me that there was an old homestead not far from town that was for sale, and that I might try my hand at farming. He told me that if that didn't work for me, I might want to try doing something else.

I had just come from a big city and didn't know the first thing about farming, but I was willing to try as I wasn't having any luck with any other work in town. Maybe that was where I needed to be and what I needed to do.

The next day I bought the homestead and moved in. I had also bought different pieces of farming equipment that I was told I would need.

That night I sat down and wrote a letter to Mother, Father and Emma, telling them where I was at, and what I was about to do. I also told Emma that it wouldn't be long and I would be sending for her.

The next day I made a trip into town with an old wagon and a horse that I had also bought the day before. When I walked into the post office, I told the woman that I wanted to mail two letters. She told me that the mail was slow and that it might be a couple of months before whoever I was sending the letters to could get a reply back to me. I told her that was okay. Standing there in front of her, I was confused as the mail was much faster than it was when I was a kid, but I accepted what she said anyway.

From the post office I went to a clothing store to buy some work clothes. The only thing I owned were suits. This was not appropriate clothing for me, being a farmer. In the store was a nice, pretty lady who was friendly.

"Can I help you?" she asked as I smiled at her.

"Yes, you can. I have arrived here from Philadelphia and the only clothes I own are similar to what I am wearing. Is there a way that you can help me pick out different clothes as I am going to be farming," I said.

"Yes, I will be happy to help you," she said, being very obliging.

"Thank you. My name is Albert," I told her.

"My name is Beth," she replied.

In my mind Beth was a pretty name, and she helped me find what I needed for my new occupation.

I left the store and walked to my wagon, where I got in and left to go back home. My day was done in town. I was ready for a hot supper of ham and beans. Then a night of sleep.

—2—

NEW OCCUPATION

The following morning I was awake and outside before the sun came up. I had gone to the corral to bridle my horse as I was going to use him to pull the big plow, to get the soil ready for planting. When the sun came up, it was very hot and time for me to rest and drink plenty of water. I even took some that I got from my well and poured it over my head.

Each day was the same and a challenge as I continued to work with my horse, pulling the plow and then planting the seeds to see if a crop would grow in the soil. This went on for a couple of months. Meanwhile, I was waiting to hear back from my parents and Emma.

Every day I went into town and I stopped by the post office to check and see if there was anything for me in general delivery. Each day I got told that there was nothing. I had been there for a couple of months and didn't understand why my parents or Emma hadn't written me back.

That particular day I walked past the clothing store again and saw Beth putting a newly sewn dress on a mannequin. I stopped and waved at her, and she waved and smiled back. So I went into the store.

"Hello, Albert," Beth said.

"Good morning, Beth. Would you like to join me for a cup of coffee?" I asked.

"Yes, I can close the shop long enough to do that. I would love to," she replied, again smiling at me.

She walked out the door, locking it behind her, and we went to the small diner where I had eaten when I first came to town.

"How do you like it here now?" Beth asked.

"I do like this town. Everyone here is friendly and helpful. My crops are starting to grow. It looks like I might be a pretty good farmer after all," I replied, laughing.

"I am happy that you are satisfied with the town that you chose to live in," Beth said with a serious look.

"Me too. This town is much different than city life. It is calmer and slower than Philadelphia was. Something that I had dreamed about for years," I said.

"We knew you would like it here," Beth commented.

"I have some beans cooking, and if you would like to come to supper, I would love to have you eat with me. it does get lonely out there," I responded.

"I will close my store early and be there at your place by 5:00 p.m.," Beth said.

We had finished our coffee and after walking her back to her store, I was on my way to my farm to make sure that the beans and ham were cooking in the pot, and to wait for Beth to arrive. While I was on my way home, I couldn't help thinking about some of the words that she had said. The reply back to me when she said, "I am happy that you are satisfied with the town that you chose to live in," and also the words, "We knew you would like it here" kind of stuck in my mind.

Not knowing if I was overreacting or that it sounded something like what I had heard before somewhere else.

Beth was a nice woman who wanted to be my friend and come here to visit and eat supper with me.

In a couple of hours there was a knock on the door and Beth had arrived.

"Come in, Beth. I am happy that you took me up on this. I haven't eaten supper with anyone for quite a while now," I spoke.

"It's quite all right, Albert. Thank you for asking me,"

Beth remarked.

I smiled again at her and watched as she gathered the plates from the counter to place the beans and ham on that we were having for supper. It was time to eat.

As we sat there eating, I felt like I had known her for years. I had a new friend. When we were done with our meal, she took our plates and went to the sink to wash and dry the dishes for me.

We talked longer before she said that she needed to return to her home. I walked her out to her horse and buggy, helping her climb into it, and then gave her the reins. Before she left, she said, "I'm happy that this was your chosen place to live."

Instead of reading more into what she had just said, I smiled at her and thanked her for saying that. Once again, it was time to sleep. I had a lot to do the next day.

In the morning I walked out to my field, where I was growing corn. The stalks were getting tall and it wouldn't be long and it would be time to harvest everything that I was growing.

—3—

CAN'T GO BACKWARD

More days passed and more trips into town. I had gone again, looking for a reply back from my parents and Emma, and once again I was told that there was nothing for me in the mail. I knew that Mother and Father wouldn't have forgotten about me, but continued to wonder if Emma had found someone else. Maybe it was time to let go of her and move on with my life.

I continued to go see Beth at her store, and she had made several trips out to my farm to help me. We were becoming very good friends, and with all of the rejections from the lady at the post office, I was ready to quit going there for a while.

One night we had a terrible wind storm. It was blowing branches all over the place, and also trees were laying on the roads leading to town. That night I heard a knock at my door. It was late and I was wondering who it could be coming to see me at that hour of the day.

When I opened the door, I saw Beth standing there. She was shivering and asked if she could come in. She told me that she was frightened by the storm and had to get out of her home. I told her that she was welcome to stay the night, if she wished. I told her that she could sleep in my bed and I would sleep on the sofa. Beth said that would be fine, so we both went to different places to rest.

After she saw how kind I was and a gentleman, she started

coming over to my home more. She had also introduced me to many of the surrounding farmers and ranchers, and I was getting to know many other people in town.

We had even gone to a meeting in the town, where all of the farmers appeared and talked about things relating to farming and their crops, or whatever they grew.

Beth told me that whenever I came to town, to come by her store and she would buy me coffee this time at the diner. That made me laugh and we were getting closer. Because of Beth, I was starting to forget about Emma.

At times she would come to the field, where she would ride my horse as it pulled the plow that I was pushing. This made it easier for me to work the soil, to get it ready for planting.

A couple of weeks later, I had bought a ring and went to her store. When I entered, she asked me if I was ready to go get something to drink or eat from the diner, and I told her that I had a question for her.

"Beth, I know that we haven't known each other for long, but when we did meet, I couldn't stay away from you. You and I have become very good friends as you have helped me till the soil, and other things that you didn't have to do. The question to you, Beth, is 'Will you be my wife?' " I asked.

Beth looked at me and smiled again. "Yes, Albert, I would be honored to marry you. What took you so long asking me?" she said.

We both stood there, laughing, and then she wanted to know if we could still go to the diner and get coffee and eat. I was so in love with this beautiful woman and very happy. I told her yes, and we walked out the door. My life was complete now.

Months passed and we stood in the church before our friends and said vows that we both meant and would keep. Beth was now my wife.

The crops were harvested and we had some money in the bank. We decided to buy some livestock and not just farm. We were going to be ranchers as well. Just because we had done well, we wanted to do better.

One night after supper, as we sat on the sofa, I told Beth about my mother and her tea parties, Father and his meat store, and how I had learned how to be a butcher working for him. I even told her about Emma.

I also said that someday we would take the train and go back to Philadelphia to visit them, and how I wanted to show her off to all my friends, Mother, Father, and even Emma. Then, as I talked, she said the strangest thing to me that left me speechless and wondering what she meant.

"Albert, we can't go backward now."

"What do you mean, Beth? We can do anything that we choose to do," I replied.

"Not now, Albert. You chose your life when you stopped here that day, when you walked off the train. I chose my life years ago, and now we are where we wanted to be and we won't be able to go back," Beth replied.

Feeling confused at what she had just told me, I got up off the sofa to go outside for a while. I had been curious from the day that I chose this town to be my home, and I wanted my parents to be included in it. I had no choice but to accept what Beth said as she was my life now.

A couple of years had passed and Beth had given birth to our son, Paul. Leaving didn't matter to me anymore as I had everything that I wanted and needed right here.

There were many days when Beth had taken Paul to work with her. I couldn't take him to the field with me while I pushed a plow. It was even getting harder for her to have him there at the store as he had grown and was walking all over. When someone came in her store to buy something, she had to watch him and make sure that he didn't leave when the door was opened. So she put a "For Sale" sign on the door and became a full-time wife and mother.

With each day in mind getting better, I felt like I was living a dream.

Paul was growing and had now turned five. He was not just walking behind Beth and me in the field, but also picking up sticks or other objects that the wind had blown on the ground.

That winter we got hit with snow and cold weather. Some of the livestock died, and some of the hay that I grew was showing signs of mold. Beth and I had spent many days chopping wood for the fireplace, in order for all of us to be warm. There was talk in town that some people had even passed away from pneumonia and typhoid fever was an epidemic again. It already had taken a lot of lives. We were worried about Paul and needed to keep him well and safe.

One day, when I returned home from going into town, I found Beth lying on the floor, covered in sweat. When I turned her over, she looked pale and was having trouble breathing. I picked her up and laid her on our bed. I covered her with many blankets and found rags to wash her with. I used cold water to try to cool her down. I knew that the doctor would be hard to find as he was busy helping other people. So it was up to me to help her and watch over Paul, too.

Several days passed and Beth wasn't getting better. I needed help with Paul, and I knew of an old woman in town who was very fond of Beth. The only thing that I knew to do was to get the horse and wagon, wrap Paul in warm blankets, and see if this woman would come out here to help me.

When I arrived at her home, she was more than willing to take the chance of getting typhoid fever and be here to help with Paul and also to help with Beth. The snow was still coming down and I was feeling overwhelmed.

When we returned to the house, I went to the bedroom to check on Beth. I was too late as she had passed away. All I could do was stand there and scream at the top of my lungs. Paul was crying and the old woman was comforting him, as well as me.

After I took the woman back home the next morning, I was outside, building a box to put Beth in, and digging a hole that was big enough for the box to fit into. I was cold and bitter.

Months passed and the snow had finally melted. At

times, again I thought about my parents and wondered if they were still alive, and I wondered again why they had chosen not to write to me.

That year the crops did survive.

—4—

SADNESS AND IMAGINATION

There was a part of me that believed that Beth was still with us. At times, when I looked at Paul, I saw a tall, beautiful woman with blue eyes and blond hair smiling and looking back at me. The woman that I saw was Beth. The harder I looked, the sooner the vision in my mind went away. Some would say that I was just overworked and tired from everything that I was doing and had to do.

There were other harsh winters that Paul and I had endured. He was a strong, handsome young man who had his mother's smile. She would have been proud of him. I tried very hard to make our life a good one. We went to church on Sunday and my cooking had gotten better. Instead of my traditional ham and beans, I had learned from watching Beth how to fix many different foods for us to eat.

I wanted Paul to grow up happy, even though his mother was not with us. There were days when he wanted to run off with his friends and I let him go. I needed him to have a solid and stable mind when he was completely grown, and for him to know exactly what he wanted and where he was going with his life, unlike the way it had turned out.

More years passed and I was feeling very old from all of the hard work I had done since I had bought the homestead. My hair had turned gray, my face was wrinkled from the hot sun beating down on it every day, my bones ached, and I was very lonely for my Beth. There were even days when

I wanted to end my life and then I thought about Paul and how this would affect him and his life.

Also, when I looked into his eyes, I saw her eyes staring back at me.

More years passed, and many of the farmers were losing money on their crops and were selling their land and homes. For me, I was too old to do anything else and I wanted the homestead and land to go to Paul. I was suffering from deprivation, feeling deprived of my wife for many years, and depression had set in.

Years later, Paul married his high school sweetheart. I had given them my blessing and it was time for me to talk to him.

"Son, I am an old man now, and tired. What I want to do is to leave you and Mary the farm and ranch. Maybe I will go back to Philadelphia, where I came from. I know that you will do good, and that you and Mary will have a happy life together. I have lived my life and am ready now to move on to another one. If I can, I will write to you. All I can ask is that you understand," I said with a tear falling from my eye.

"I do understand, Father. I have watched you struggle and I see the sadness in your eyes from missing Mother. I know how hard it is on you to just get up in the morning. I promise you that Mary and I will take good care of everything here, and I won't let you down. Do whatever you choose to do, Father," Paul replied.

"I will never forget about you, son," I said.

The next day I packed a small bag and put on the same suit that I wore when I came here. My time of living in this small town was over with. Once again, I had told my family goodbye and walked to the train station. Sitting at the station was the same train I had arrived here on. I walked over to it and got on.

When I raised my head, I found myself sitting in the same seat as before. The conductor was standing there, smiling and looking at me. Many years had passed and he still looked the same. He hadn't aged like I had.

"Good day, Albert," the conductor said.

"How do you know my name?" I asked.

"Albert, we have had this discussion before, but at that time, it was as if you either didn't believe what I was telling you, or you refused to understand what I was saying. As you know, you are an old man now, and maybe you will now listen to my words that I am saying to you," he said.

"Why am I the only one riding this train?" I asked.

"Albert, you have been on this train with us for many years. You see, this train is for people who are undecided about their life. Each time that you decided to get off at a station, it was only in your imagination as you never left your seat. You have been creating your life in your mind. You created a life with yourself in Philadelphia, and before that it was a different place.

"There are other passengers on here that you choose not to see, just as they choose not to see you. All of you, from the very start of your life, have been unsure about what you wanted, or where you wanted to be. Each one of you did create a good life for yourself, but when you imagined something bad happening to you or to someone that you had created, you didn't want to be there any longer. The old man that you have seen getting on this train is you. That is why the man doesn't talk to you. Who you have talked to and imagined isn't real, Albert," the conductor remarked.

"Then why does it all feel real?" I asked.

"Because you are writing your own story of your life in your mind. When you are ready, again there will be another place in your mind that you will want to be at, and you will once again leave the train. You want the perfect life and the perfect place to live , where there are no problems or confusion. This place has always brought each of you back to reality as, eventually, you need to leave the life that you are imagining.

"There is no perfect life, Albert, and all of you here haven't and won't see this, so you continue to live in your own world, creating and imagining what you want your life to be like. Every one of you have continued to stay on this train and none of you have gotten off," he said.

I sat there, watching the conductor walk away. I wondered how I had gotten here in the first place, and why I had lived a lifetime on this train. Many things were explained to me. The reason why I didn't hear back from the people I wanted to be my parents, and the girl that I wanted as my wife, was because they were not real. Beth and Paul were not real. Nothing was what I believed it to be. My being an old man now, I would continue to sit on this train, searching for a town that didn't exist.

When I read the last words of my grandfather's book, I closed it, walking to the door to turn off the light switch, shut the door, and walked down a long hall leading to the front door.

My name is Albert Weatherton Jr., and I am on my way to visit my grandfather in a nursing home. After reading his story and his words, I am wondering if I exist, or am I a figment of Grandfather's imagination as he sits on a train, going nowhere.

PART V

THE FACE BEHIND THE MASK

—1—
AWKWARD MEETING

I drove the coast on a Saturday morning with "KISS" blaring on the radio, and the people passing me were giving me a "thumbs up" because they liked the music I chose to listen to. With the sun shining brightly, I was ready to meet a woman I had been messaging on line.

My name is Ellie Bowen. I was born in a small town in Colorado. When I was 14, my parents and I made a trip to San Francisco, where my father had a job interview. He had gotten a call from the owner of a big bank, asking him if he would be willing to relocate from the small town we lived in, to work in the city. At that time, Father told the man that he would need to discuss this with Mother first, before he could give an answer. Also, he would need to go there to speak with the man directly and see the bank he would be working for.

The man told Father that would be fine. That evening, Father did speak to Mother about the move and they agreed that it would be a consideration, and a trip to San Francisco was planned.

Two weeks later, we were on the highway going west. When we arrived here, we saw the large city, which was something that none of us had seen before. Mother and Father talked about the change that would happen in my life if they did move here with me.

When Father went to the tall, large bank where he would work, to meet with the owner, he discussed his concerns with him. After finding out that the owner also came from a small town before moving here with his family, and how much they learned to love it, Father then told him that he would take the job.

Within a couple of months we had gone from being country folk to city people.

For me it was a good decision as I like it here. I love the beach, the ocean, surfing, and all of the friends that I have made. I have no desire to go back to where we started from. When Father retired, he and Mother went back to Colorado, where their roots would always be. But for me, I had no interest in leaving and made San Francisco my home.

Being employed with a large firm, and making more money than I needed, I was satisfied to stay right where I was.

A couple of months ago, I got a friend request from a woman on a social media site. At first I was somewhat hesitant to accept her request, but eventually I did. She sounded like an interesting person to get to know. A couple of days ago, she asked me to come to her home in Santa Barbara, where we could meet and get to know each other.

Her name is Sandy Young. She is working for a firm and her job is similar to mine, so this is something that we did have in common. She told me that she was getting out of a bad relationship she had been in. She said that she was ready to meet new people and move on with her life.

I explained to her that I currently wasn't in a relationship, but did have a good friend that I had known for years that I trusted and did enjoy being around, and that his name was Brock Freeman. Most women who look at him say that he is handsome, and others think that he is "hot." We had been good friends since I was hired by the same company that we work for.

Someday, maybe, we can take our friendship to the relationship status.

So with the windows down and me still singing to the radio, I was ready for a day of fun. Santa Barbara was my last stop until I drove back home. The exit sign let me know that I needed to turn off of the interstate in half a mile, and it was time to slow my car down.

After driving through some of the city, I was able to locate Sandy's home. It was in an expensive neighborhood and larger than what I had imagined. After I drove up her drive and was walking to the front door, I heard arguing coming from inside of the house. With this happening, I questioned myself on whether I should turn around and leave.

Then my thoughts were to knock, to see if the arguing would stop and someone would know that I was waiting outside.

The arguing was getting intense and it was more than time for it to be interrupted.

"Gerald, I don't know what I saw that day. It could have been an animal lying on the floor, for all I know. At this point it really doesn't matter."

"Sandy, it does matter. I know that you are mad at me, but we need to figure this out together. I have told you that I am sorry, and that is all I can do because you won't allow me to move back in here in order for me to show you," Gerald replied.

"You should have thought about what you did to me before you did it. And another thing. Tell your girlfriend to stop calling me and hanging up. I know that it is her doing this," said Sandy.

"For the last time, Sandy, I am telling you the truth, I have no girlfriend. I have always loved you, and I am sorry that woman won't leave you alone. She won't leave me alone either. I don't want anything to do with her, and I wish that you would believe me!" Gerald yelled.

"Gerald, I told you to get out as I have company coming

over. Leave now!" Sandy responded.

"It didn't take you long to find someone else!" Gerald said harshly.

"It's a woman, and none of your business, you jerk!" Sandy screamed back at him.

By then, I could see that it was time to knock louder as neither one of them had heard me the first time. So instead of knocking lightly, I pounded on the door.

"She is here now, Gerald! Get out now!" Sandy said, once again screaming at him.

It wasn't long and the front door opened and Gerald was on his way out.

"Sandy, we aren't done talking about this!" Gerald screamed back at her.

He had the last word, and walking behind him was Sandy. "You must be Ellie. I am sorry for the way that Gerald screamed in your ear when he was leaving."

"It's okay. Yes, I am Ellie," I responded.

"Please come in," Sandy said.

"Is this man the one that you were telling me about?" I asked as we walked to her sofa.

"Yes, that was him. He won't accept the reality that we are no longer together. Every day now it is the same argument. There have been many times when I walk through my front door and see him sitting here, wanting to talk to me. I don't have anything nice to say to him now. All I want him to do is just leave me alone as I have told him this a thousand times, and it does me no good," she said.

"Have you thought about changing your locks, getting a watch dog, or hiring someone to watch you and your house?" I asked.

"I have thought about all of that, Ellie, but the one thing that I do know about him is that he would still find a way in here to talk to me," she replied.

"Then how are you going to get rid of him?" I asked.

"I have a plan, and I would like to know if you would like to be a part of it. In a couple of weeks I have scheduled a getaway to go to my beach home in Santa Cruz. I would like some company. It will be fun as there is a lot to do. If you want, you can meet me. With my being away from here, I am hoping that he will get the rest of his things out of here, and maybe he will go back to the woman that he swears up and down that he doesn't want anything to do with."

"It all sounds like fun. I have a week of vacation that I can take in a couple of weeks. It would give me a chance to see Santa Cruz as I have always wanted to go there. Hopefully, your plan works where Gerald is concerned, if this is really what you want," I said.

"It is, Ellie. I will tell you more about all of this when we are on our vacation," she said.

Sandy and I spent the rest of the day talking about other things. This vacation would give me the time I needed away from work, and the time she needed away from her job and Gerald. The day had progressed and it was time for me to leave and return to my home.

The traffic was light, so my drive back was faster. When I walked through my front door, I saw that I had a missed call. The call came from Brock, asking me to call him back.

"Hello," Brock said.

"Hello, Brock. It's me calling you back," I replied.

"Yes, Ellie. Where were you today? I went to your home to see if you wanted to have a late night dinner with me tonight," he responded.

"I went to Santa Barbara today to visit a friend. I would love to have dinner with you tonight," I replied.

"I will see you then in a couple of hours, after I finish up some paperwork that I am doing," Brock said.

One of the things that I loved about him was that he was always coming up with romantic ideas. Like, for instance, a late night dinner date. When he did arrive, I would share my day with him before he brought me back home.

When he did come to get me and we had arrived at the restaurant, I saw that it was expensive and beautiful. Inside, the ceiling was made of glass, and everyone in there could look up at the stars and the moon. The owners had named it "Moon Beam."

The waitress had come to take our order and brought us a bottle of white wine that Brock had ordered. When she left the table, I told him that I was ready to tell him more of what my day had been like.

"I had a wonderful drive down the coast. I went to meet a woman that I met on line from a social media site. We have been messaging back and forth for a couple of months now. When I found her home, I was surprised as it is in an expensive neighborhood and larger than she had explained to me. After I parked my car, and was walking up the front steps leading to the door, I overheard her and her ex-boyfriend talking, or should I say *screaming,* at each other.

"Not knowing if I should leave and come back later, or knock, I chose to go ahead and knock. Neither one of them heard me. They were focused on yelling at each other. I stood there and listened to their conversation for a while, and then I decided to pound on the door to get a response. My friend heard the knock and again told Gerald to leave. When he did, as he was walking out the door, he informed her that he would be back and that their conversation wasn't over with yet.

"After that, Sandy invited me into her home, letting me know that he is the one she had told me about. In a couple of weeks, she is going to her beach house, and I got an invite to meet her there. I am wondering if this is a wise thing to do right now. I haven't been to Santa Cruz and I do have some vacation time coming to me, so maybe I should stop over-thinking this and join her," I explained.

"Ellie, it sounds like you had quite an experience today. I wonder if you are doing the smart thing by going there with a woman that you just met. What are your plans if her ex-boyfriend decides to join her at a later date? He might not be a nice guy when it comes to you being there," Brock said.

"If he does show up, and all they want to do is argue, I will leave and come home. You are right as I really don't know Sandy that well. Hopefully, everything goes good on this vacation, and she is the friend that I think that she is," I replied.

When the waitress brought our food, we laughed and talked about work. Our night out had gone by quickly, and soon Brock would be taking me home.

The next day, I was on my way to work to talk to my boss about taking time off. I was questioning myself on whether I should go. Not knowing what was going to happen at Santa Cruz, I was wondering if Sandy's worst nightmare with everything that was happening in her life right now might be getting ready to show its ugly head. No matter what, this was a chance that I was willing to take.

—2—

TAKING A CHANCE

When I walked into the office where I worked, I went to my CEO to speak to him about taking time off. As I suspected, it wasn't going to be a problem, so the plan was in motion.

After I arrived home, I called Sandy to let her know that I would meet her in Santa Cruz in a couple of weeks. She gave me directions to her beach home.

Around 7:00 p.m. Brock came by to bring me some papers that I had forgotten to bring home from the meeting that all of us had that day. I was busy with a client and had left my office for the day, forgetting to grab the paperwork from my desk.

"Ellie, did Tom approve your time off in a couple of weeks?" Brock asked.

"Yes, he did. Since we talked last night, I have been thinking about what you said. One day of meeting Sandy and talking with her really isn't enough time to get to know someone. Hopefully, this vacation is fun for her and me. The reason why she wants to take this vacation is to give Gerald the chance to get all of his things out of her home. She is also hoping that he goes back to the woman he was with when he cheated on her."

"Just be careful, Ellie. This situation that she is involving you in could go bad. Remember, this trip is focused around you going there to have fun, which means that if you choose not to be around her all of the time, that is okay. I am sure that you and I will be talking on the phone while you are there. If you need me, call," Brock replied.

In Santa Barbara, Sandy had another phone call from an unknown number. This call was like several that she had received. She heard breathing on the other end, but no one would talk. She was upset and had called Gerald to tell him to come to her home ASAP.

"Gerald, I know that your girlfriend is the one calling me. This is getting old, and you need to tell her to stop bothering me! She wants you, and I don't anymore, so go back to her and then I can have some peace again!" she said.

"I will tell her to leave you alone, but she won't even leave me alone. I have told her that I am in love with you, and she still is insisting that we slept together. I don't believe it. I just want to come back home, Sandy," he said.

"That is never going to happen, and you know it. Get the rest of your things out of here, and give me back my key," Sandy said.

"No! We have to work this out!"

"There is no way that we can," Sandy responded.

Gerald left and she was calling me to tell me that they had another fight. She said that because of this, she was looking forward to time away. Of course, I told her that I was, too, for other reasons.

The next two weeks went faster than I thought they would and my excitement of going to Santa Cruz was becoming stronger. I had packed a bag and was walking to my car to leave for some fun in the sun.

Whereas at Sandy's home, Gerald had come by again to talk to her.

"Gerald, why are you showing up here again today, un-invited? I needed to talk to you the other day, but I have said all that I need to say. I keep telling you to stay away, but yet you persist in coming here all the time. We are not together anymore," Sandy said.

"I know that you are mad, but with time you will get over

it. I saw your bag when I walked through the door. Where are you going?" he asked.

"That is none of your business. Yes, I was sad at the beginning. Actually, I was more hurt than anything, but that has changed now. I am telling you again to not come here unless I call you to. I need to leave now, and where I am going is not your concern. I don't want to find you here when I get back," she said loudly.

"I will never be out of your life. You will see that all of this is a mistake. I know you will want me back again. I will keep the key for when you do," he commented.

"If I need to change the locks, I will," she spoke as she walked out of the house with her bag.

Gerald continued to stand in the doorway with what Sandy thought was a crazed look on his face.

"I love you. I will be waiting for you. See you soon," he said.

Sandy couldn't wait to drive away from there. She was afraid that because of Gerald trying to convince her that he was totally innocent, maybe some way he was going crazy. While driving, she found a note that read, "I am watching you and waiting." As she read this, she threw it on the floor of her car. She believed that it was a note from Gerald. Instead of going back to confront him with this, she continued to drive toward Santa Cruz.

Within a few hours, I had arrived at Sandy's beach home. She had pulled her car in behind mine as we both had gotten there at the same time. Her home wasn't far from the beach, and people were walking around in bathing suits, with towels wrapped around their waists. I could see the ocean, and for a minute I stood and watched the waves as they came up on the shore. I smiled as the fun had already begun.

"Ellie, I am happy that you were able to join me," Sandy said.

"Thank you for inviting me. I have always loved the beach and the ocean," I replied.

"I have lived in California my entire life and I never get

tired of coming here. I even brought my surf board," she said.

"Me too! I can't wait to get started," I replied.

"Then let's go into my beach home, change, and ride some waves," she said.

It wasn't long and we were in our suits and walking to the water with our boards. It had been a while since I had surfed, but it didn't take me long and I was riding the waves with the best of the surfers, including Sandy.

After a couple of hours, we decided to walk back to the house and shower, then dress for dinner at a restaurant that was not far from there.

"Thanks for inviting me," I told her.

"I am happy that you could join me, Ellie. I haven't been here in a while, and I needed a break. Gerald and I came here many times in the two years that we were together. With all of the arguing that we have been doing, it was time for me to have an escape. With each conversation that we have, it turns into a fight. I have told him to get the rest of his things and for him to return my house keys, and he still believes that somehow I will forgive him, and that isn't going to happen.

"Today he came back to my home again and saw my bag on the floor. He wanted to know where I was going, and of course I told him that it was none of his business. I'm sure he thinks in his sick mind that I am meeting a man somewhere. He said that he will never be out of my life, and as I was walking to my car, he was standing at the door, telling me that he loves me and that he will be waiting for my return. He sounded crazy and had a crazed look on his face.

"I couldn't wait to get out of there quick enough. While I was driving here, I found a note from him on the seat that said he was watching me and waiting. He had typed the note, but because of our arguments, I suspect it came from him. With him telling me this, I am sure that he won't be here this week to spoil our fun," Sandy said.

"Wow! It doesn't sound to me like he is going to give up on you that easy. You might still think about getting a watch dog, or someone to keep an eye on you and the house," I said.

"I told him that when I get back, if I need to change the door locks, that I would. Also, not to come over unannounced again. I am still getting phone calls from that number that isn't registering, and the person isn't talking when I answer. I have no doubt that it is his girlfriend just trying to stir up more arguments between us, and I have asked him to tell her to stop. He needs to go be with her, as I don't know how much more of this I can take. He says he isn't with her and I have no idea where he is staying when he leaves my home," she replied.

After our conversation about Gerald, our food had been brought to our table on the patio, where we could see the stars. We ate and stopped talking about Gerald, switching to a different conversation that was pleasant to talk about.

When we left, we took a different route to the beach home. The moon was bright and again the night appeared to be calm. Just before we returned to her home, I saw a shadow of a person that appeared to be following us. It appeared to be this way, but with all the people who were walking up and down the beach, I didn't want to plant something in Sandy's mind that may not be there, so I said nothing.

After we had walked inside her home, I told her that it was time for me to unpack my clothes and then go to bed, to get ready for the next day of fun. She said that she needed to do the same thing. That was the end of the first day and night there. We had more days and nights of fun waiting to happen.

—3—

WAITING AND WATCHING

The next morning I called Brock before he went to work, to let him know that so far everything was fine.

"Good morning," Brock said.

"Good morning to you, too," I said.

"How are things going at Santa Cruz?" he asked.

"Everything is fine so far. We went surfing yesterday and ate out last night. She told me more about some things that Gerald had told her in their arguments, and what she had told him. Today, so far, his name hasn't been mentioned. I will keep you informed and whether he shows up here. She thinks that he won't be coming," I said.

"That's good, Ellie. With everything that has happened with them, be aware of your surroundings. Call me in a couple of days, or sooner, and let me know how you are doing," he said.

"Okay, I will," I responded.

What we didn't know was that Gerald had continued to stay in Sandy's home in Santa Barbara and was going through her things to find out where she had gone. While he was doing this, the phone rang and he didn't answer it, but did hear her boss telling her that if she needed to take off more time for her vacation in Santa Cruz, that it was okay, and to let him know and he would approve it. This was the information that he was looking for.

The more he thought about where she had gone, the

more jealous he became as he was convinced that she was seeing another man or she would have taken him back.

After we drank our coffee, we were almost ready to start our day.

"I hope that you slept well," Sandy said.

"I did, and thank you. What do you want to do today?" I asked.

"I thought that we could walk around on the boardwalk and look through all of the stores. I'm sure that you would enjoy this. I haven't been here in a while and it will be interesting for me as well. There are places there where we can go to eat lunch. Then, later in the day if you want, we can go surfing again," she replied.

"Yes, that sounds like fun," I responded.

After a while, we were leaving. There was a huge carousel and amusement park there that I wanted to see as well.

After my conversation with Brock, he had made arrangements to come to Santa Cruz to keep an eye on me. I guess that he was worried that I would be having so much fun that I wouldn't see danger if it was there. This would happen with his arrival this weekend.

In Santa Barbara, Gerald was pacing Sandy's floor, stewing over what he believed she was doing. The more he paced, the angrier he became.

As we walked around on the boardwalk, we saw people riding skateboards and bicycles. Everyone looked like they were having a good time.

After lunch, we were on our way back to the beach home. Brock was talking to our boss, and Gerald had left Sandy's house. There were things happening that we weren't aware of.

Just before we arrived at the front door of her home, I saw a person standing in a cottage across from her house. The person was looking at us through a small opening of a curtain. I couldn't tell if it was a man or a woman. This time I did bring it up to Sandy.

"Sandy, am I imagining things, or is there a person staring at us from that cottage through barely opened curtains?" I asked.

"Yes, Ellie, I can see a person. This is nothing that is unusual as there are a lot of people who come here and rent the cottages. Maybe that person is just looking around and it only appears that whoever it is may be looking at us," she replied.

"You are probably right," I said, laughing.

All of the talk that we had about Gerald may be crazy and Brock telling me to be aware of my surroundings had me consumed with things that I shouldn't be thinking about. I was here to have fun.

After we changed into our swim wear once again, we were on our way to the ocean to spend the remainder of our time out until it was dark, sailing in a boat that tourists enjoyed riding. When we returned, we got dressed for another night out, walking to the restaurant and also the tower clock. We had been gone for several hours, and when we returned, we found her front door unlocked.

"Sandy, is it normal for you to forget to lock your door?" I asked.

"There have been once, or maybe twice, when I forgot. But most of the time I am very careful about remembering to lock the door. It must be all the excitement that I am having that caused it today," she said.

When we entered, everything looked normal and so she was convinced that she had just walked away without locking it. I didn't want to make a big deal over it, so since it was midnight, we decided to go to bed.

When I opened my dresser to get my nightgown, my clothes looked like they had been rearranged. A sweater that I had brought, in case we had a cold night here on the beach, was partially sticking out of my drawer. This was not like me to do this. Then again, it wasn't like Sandy to leave her door unlocked. With this being said, maybe we both were having an off day.

In the morning, Sandy asked me if I would like some pastry to eat with our coffee. She said that there was a place close to the boardwalk and that she would be back within an hour. I told her that I would love some, so she left to walk to the donut shop.

When she walked out of the house, I went to the window to look out. I continued to see a person staring out the window of the cottage at this house. All I could see was part of someone's head. Again, my imagination was on overtime. I was happy that people walked outside around this area day and night.

After Sandy returned, I asked her to tell me the story of what had caused her and Gerald to break up. Something was going on in my mind, making me wonder if we could be in great danger.

"This might not be any of my business, but over coffee and pastry, I would like you to tell me the story about what caused you and Gerald to break up," I said.

"Sure, Ellie. I will be happy to tell you what happened. A few months ago was when I kicked him out. The first year that we were together, he liked doing things with me and was attentive to my needs. We were always going places and enjoying life together. In the second year, I felt like he was changing. He had become comfortable with our relationship.

"When we were around other women, it seemed like he was a little too nice to them for my liking. There was one woman that liked to tilt her head around him when she spoke, and she smiled a lot at him and tried to say cute things to make him laugh. I guess he liked the bimbo look. Her husband worked at a company that Gerald's company is affiliated with, and there would be times when we would see them at a company party.

"One night she called Gerald on the phone, telling him that her husband was out of town, and her car had broken down on the interstate. She said that she needed a ride after the tow truck came to get it. He was more than willing to help her. When I asked if I could go with him, he told me no, and that he would be back in a few hours or less. I sat on the sofa, waiting for him until 1:00 a.m. Finally, being exhausted,

I went to bed.

"The next morning when he walked through the door, carrying his shoes, hoping that I was still in bed sleeping, he saw me sitting and waiting for him. I asked him what took so long, and he told me that they had waited for the tow truck and that it didn't show up until that morning. He said that he slept in his car. I could see that his hair was messed up some. He had pink lipstick on his face. His shirt didn't look the way it did when he walked out the door, and he was carrying his suit jacket that, at the time, smelt like perfume. It wasn't mine.

"I told him what I saw and he had all kinds of excuses. Finally, I got tired of hearing them, so I dropped the conversation, not wanting to hear the worst.

"After that, Gerald started coming home later and hardly showing me the attention that I thought I deserved. His excuse was that he was tired and that he just wanted to go to sleep.

"Then he told me that he would be gone for a couple of days because the company he worked for was sending him to a convention, and that wives or girlfriends weren't invited. He said that the men might party some alone, and none of them wanted to be nagged the whole time. I told him that it wasn't a big deal to me. Oh, yes, he was partying all right!

"The next day I had packed a bag for him with his nicest clothes and had to ask him for a kiss just before he walked out the door. Things had really changed for us, and not in a good way. All I wanted was for him to talk to me about it.

"I had some shopping to do that day, and so after Gerald left, I was on my way to the store when I got stuck at a traffic light. It was taking forever to turn green, and so I was sitting and waiting in my car, looking around. By chance, I happened to see Gerald holding the door open for the same woman that he had gone to rescue on the interstate that night. He took her bag from the sidewalk and put it on his back seat. After he did that, he got in his car and drove away. Neither one of them saw me, and I felt lied to, and betrayed.

"When he did return to my home, I told him what I saw

and that I knew that he had been lying and cheating on me for months. Also, that I wanted him and his things out of my house, and to never come back. He told me that it wasn't his fault that he had been asked to pick her up at that spot. She said that she was going to the convention to surprise her husband, even though he had told her that she couldn't go. So she had called Gerald for a ride as her car was still in the shop, getting fixed, and she didn't want to call a taxi.

"Finally, he did leave and I didn't see him for about a week. During that time, I had gone to this woman's home to talk to her, to tell her that Gerald was all hers and that I wanted nothing to do with him any longer. When I walked up to the door, I heard the woman and a man fighting, and so I went to the window to look inside, as their conversation was heated, and then it stopped abruptly. I saw something lying on the floor and I couldn't tell what it was, other than the woman was standing over it. I turned around and left to go home.

"When Gerald did show up at my home, he said that the woman told him she would move in with him, and he said he told her that he wanted to be with me and had refused her. Also, he mentioned that the woman was following him and not giving up on him.

"He also said that she had told him that the night at the convention, she said that they had slept together in his room. He said that he would never cheat on me and that he knew that he had been tricked and that nothing had happened between them that night.

"She had told him that her husband was dangerous, and that she wanted nothing to do with him again. Her husband had found out that she had slept with Gerald and left home.

"He said that he told her that she'd better get her husband to come back as he wanted nothing to do with her. He said he had been staying in different motels to try to get away from her, and that she wasn't giving him up.

"With all of the lies that he had told me while we were together, I found it hard to believe anything that came out of his mouth. I just told him to leave me alone and get his stuff out and to go back to her.

"For a while after that, I didn't see him and then he started coming around again with the same lies as before, and it was the same argument all the time. I told him that I had gone to her home and seen something, lying on the floor, and that I left when I saw whatever it was with her standing over it, and that I had gone there to tell her to keep him. For some reason he wants to know what I saw on the floor, and I keep telling him that I don't know.

"Then I decided that I needed to occupy my mind, so I signed up for a social media site, where you and I met. I keep getting phone calls when I am home, and whoever it is won't stop. This is why I had to come here for a while, Ellie. I had to find some peace again," Sandy said.

"It sounds like Gerald was trying to be very convincing, and wanted you to believe whatever he told you," I replied.

"I am happy that you decided to come here to be with me," she said.

"I needed the time away from my job as well, Sandy. Before I met you, my plans were to go to Hawaii for a week. I am glad that I came here. I didn't realize how interesting and fun Santa Cruz is. It is much bigger than I thought it would be. There is so much action outside, day and night. This was a place that I thought that Brock and I would see together for the first time. There is a part of me that misses him," I said.

"It sounds like you have a good guy. At one time, I thought Gerald was a good guy. If you didn't come here to be with me, I would be afraid to do anything as I would be thinking that he would show up. It looks to me like he is staying in Santa Barbara, waiting, or he would have been here by now," she responded.

I knew that Sandy thought everything was under control. She was the one that had the relationship with him, and maybe she was right about him. I was still not convinced that she did, and that she might be sticking her head in the sand, not wanting to admit to herself that this guy was capable of anything and everything.

—4—

ON THE BOARDWALK

When we finished eating, we had another day of fun planned. We were going back to the ocean to swim and surf. I knew that Sandy was a tip-top surfer, but I hadn't seen her swim much yet.

As we left the beach home, I saw a woman walking out the door of the cottage across from Sandy's home. She was wearing a scarf and sunglasses. I was somewhat confused with this as it was a beautiful day with no wind. That day the sun was shining brighter than I had seen it shine since we had been here.

Since Santa Cruz was a place where a lot of tourists enjoyed going, I just chocked it up to being a woman staying there that might have come from either a different country or state. Maybe she was leaving for the day and wanted to dress for any weather that might change. At least I knew now that the person looking through the window with the curtains spread apart some was just a woman, and not Gerald.

We had made a detour on the way to the beach. She wanted to show me another route from the boardwalk that led to the beach. Sandy said that there weren't very many people that took it because of the high tide at times that came up on the shore below it. Today was a good day to go that route as the tide was low.

As we were walking, I noticed the same woman that

came from the cottage making every turn that we made. There were so many people walking around that I couldn't tell if she was following us or just maybe going somewhat in the same direction that we were going. Finally, we were standing below the boardwalk, looking at the other side. I couldn't see her, so again attributed it to being a coincidence.

As we walked back to the beach where Sandy and I chose to swim, there were many people that had the same idea. The beach was packed and it looked like another day of doing what I loved to do.

Sandy and I had been in the ocean several times and I could see that she was a great swimmer. Apparently, living in California her whole life and being a beach kid was the reason why. I took a break and came back to shore to sit on my blanket. I had stopped watching Sandy and instead was just wanting some time alone.

As I was sitting there, enjoying this and rubbing sun screen on, I heard a woman that was standing on the beach scream. She saw Sandy's head bobbing up and down in the water. When I, too, saw this, the lifeguard was already running to the water to rescue her.

When he brought her back to the shore, she was gasping for air. He asked her what happened and she said that she didn't know. One minute she was swimming, and then she said that she felt something sharp that had jabbed her in the leg, and her body had gone limp and she couldn't swim. She looked at her leg and saw nothing.

"Sandy, are you all right? Do you want to sit here for a while, or go to a hospital?" I asked.

"No, Ellie. I will be fine in a while. I don't know what happened or what it was that poked me. Maybe a fish just bit me," she said, laughing.

"Maybe. Do you want to go back to the beach house?" I asked.

"I will be all right. When I feel better, I would like for us to go to the amusement park again. There is a lot there that you haven't seen yet. Don't worry. I will be fine," she said.

"Okay. Then let's go have some more fun," I replied.

It was a slow walk there, but I could see that Sandy was all right. Whatever she had just experienced was a lesson for me to be careful when I was swimming in the ocean. For all I knew, she might have gotten jabbed by a syringe needle.

With so many people also at the amusement park, we had to wait in line several times. Both of us were having fun again and the swimming scare was a thing of the past.

Once again I noticed the same woman that had come out of the cottage. This time she had taken off her scarf, but still was wearing sunglasses. She stood in line not far from us, and when I smiled at her, she didn't smile back. She was alone and not friendly. I had a bad feeling about her as she acted strange. She was obviously nervous about something. She kept looking behind herself and acting skittish. I didn't want to bother Sandy with my concerns, so I just pretended like I didn't see her.

Our fun continued, and then I saw a man coming toward the strange woman. He grabbed her arm and she acted like she didn't like it. Then she gave me some kind of a look that somewhat frightened me before they walked away. Maybe she was afraid of that man. But because we were having fun, I left it alone.

For the most part, our day had been fun and we were ready to walk back to the house. This time, when we got to the front door, I looked over at the window of the cottage and the curtains were shut. I sighed with relief as it bothered me for days, feeling like we were being watched. Maybe now it was time to take a breath and relax.

That night we dressed up again to go to a different place to eat. I told Sandy that I needed to call Brock and talk to him for a while. She told me that she wasn't ready yet to leave, and that she would be by the time my phone call was over. In a couple of days, Santa Cruz was having a Mardi Gras on the boardwalk and I wanted to invite Brock to go with us. Our time here was almost done, and this would be something that Brock would love to do as well.

"Hello," Brock said.

"Brock, it's Ellie," I replied.

"I know who you are, silly girl," he said, chuckling.

"I called to let you know that we are still okay. We did have a scare today at the beach. Sandy was swimming and I had taken a break. I heard a scream from a woman and saw the lifeguard running over to get Sandy out of the water. Her head was bobbing up and down. She said that it felt like her leg got poked with a sharp object, and then she said that her body went limp. She thought maybe she had gotten bit by a fish. I am concerned for fear of it being a syringe needle," I said.

"Did you take her to the hospital to get checked out?" he asked.

"No, she didn't want to go. We sat on the beach and after a while, she wanted to go to the amusement park. She assured me that she was all right. Tonight we are going out to dinner again."

"Was there anyone around her when she was having problems in the ocean?" Brock asked.

"There were all kinds of people swimming," I replied.

"I'm happy your friend is all right, Ellie," Brock said.

"Me too. The main reason why I called you is to let you know that, so far, everything is going good and there haven't been any signs of Gerald. Not even a phone call. In a couple of days, Santa Cruz is having a Mardi Gras on the board-walk, and if you want to come here, it would be fun. Sandy said that you are welcome to stay in her extra bedroom that she has," I commented.

"That sounds like a lot of fun. I was planning on leaving here tomorrow to surprise you, but something at work is going to keep me here for one more day. I would love to come there, meet your new friend, and take you both to the Mardi Gras. I am not sure exactly what time I will be there, but if it gets dark and I still haven't arrived, go ahead and go, and I will find you in the crowd. I will be wearing a mask, so you might not recognize me. As for you, Ellie, I could find you no matter what you are wearing," he said, laughing again.

I told Brock that he was very funny and that I would see him when he got here.

By the time I was off the phone, Sandy was all ready to go. When we walked out of the house, I once again looked to see if anyone was looking out the curtains. Seeing nothing, I was relieved.

The restaurant that we went to was different than any that we had seen or been to since we got there. It was shaped like a ship and the waitress and waiters were wearing pirate outfits. I was impressed as, once again, I had gone to a place that I had never been.

Sandy and I sat there and talked, and she told me that she was happy that she didn't drown in the ocean today. I told her that was a scare not just for her, but for me as well.

When I looked around the room, once again I saw the woman from the cottage. She was sitting at the bar and was checking out everything in there. I had decided that when she gave me a weird look that maybe she was just having a bad day, and so I stopped looking at her.

The waves from the ocean were splashing up on the side of the restaurant wall and the decor was unique. Sandy had done everything she possibly could do to make my vacation and hers a good once. We had gotten to know each other and had become good friends. I felt sorry for her as I knew that everything on the boardwalk and the beach house reminded her of Gerald. It had only been a few months since they broke up, and she was probably thinking about the good times that they did have there, and not saying anything for fear that she would ruin my vacation. I knew she felt deprivation because the life she thought she would have with him didn't happen.

After we ate, it was getting late and time for us to leave. I could see that woman still sitting at the bar, but when I looked that way, I tried very hard not to look directly at her.

On the way back, we talked and laughed, and when we finally reached the house, we were both exhausted from our day and it was time to sleep.

The next morning we were up early, getting ready to make the most out of what time we had at Santa Cruz. It was going to be surfing and later paddle boarding. We did this for hours, and then it was time to take a break. The city had already started setting up different booths and other things to get ready for Mardi Gras. While sitting at a table, watching the workers, it was almost the end of our vacation. For me, a return to San Francisco, and for Sandy, a return to Santa Barbara.

"Sandy, don't you think that it is odd that Gerald hasn't called you since he didn't show up here?" I asked.

"I kind of do, Ellie, but maybe he got his things and went somewhere with his girlfriend. He might have finally accepted that our relationship is over with, and he has moved on like I asked him to," she said.

"Maybe, Sandy, but as persistent as you have told me he is, it makes me wonder," I commented.

Our rest was over and we started walking through all the shops, to see what they had for costumes. Some of the owners were still putting them on the racks, and so we talked about waiting until tomorrow to buy ours. I was very excited because, for me, it would be like dressing up for Halloween when I was a child.

As we walked back to the house that day, I saw the same woman from the cottage. She appeared to be going back there as she was walking in our direction, carrying a large bag that looked heavy. Maybe she went ahead and bought her costume instead of waiting. This woman was medium size, but looked like she might work out at a gym as her arms were muscular. Her hair looked to me like it had been recently bleached, and she was wearing something over a bathing suit that a pole dancer would wear. Once again, the man that she was with was nowhere in sight.

That night we decided to order food in. It was going to be a shorter day for us. Tomorrow was going to be when a lot more people came here to participate in the celebration.

Before we returned to our rooms, the phone rang and Brock was calling.

"Hello, Brock," I said.

"Hello, Ellie. I know that I am probably calling too late, but I needed to let you know that I won't be there in time to walk you and your friend to the boardwalk for Mardi Gras. One of our clients needs to talk to me about some papers that he is signing, and this will make my day at work longer than I planned on it being," she said.

"That's fine. We can have a light dinner before you arrive, and then after you are here, maybe we can go to one of the nicer restaurants. I can't wait to see what you will be wearing," I commented.

"You won't recognize me. I'll see you tomorrow," he replied, chuckling.

Brock and I had been around each other for a number of years, so it would take a wild costume for me not to recognize him, but I would pretend and play along with him, letting him think that he could fool me.

Sandy had already gone to her room, and I was ready to go to mine. Some extra sleep would do us both some good as we had a busy, fun week, and the excitement wasn't over with yet.

In the morning, we once again were up early and on our way to the boardwalk to look through many shops, to find the perfect costume. All of the shops and stores finished putting them on racks and were displaying them in the windows for everyone to see and admire.

Some of the stores even allowed us to try them on first, before we made up our minds on what we wanted to buy. Every place was packed with people. We had even seen two ladies fighting over the same costume. We stood back, laughed, and stayed away from them.

After a morning of shopping, we found a small café where we had a light lunch. We would wait on Brock to arrive before we ate dinner.

After we ate, our lunch, we returned to the amusement

park for the last time, to enjoy more fun. I had a great time at Santa Cruz and was happy that Sandy had asked me to join her.

Late afternoon we returned to the beach house. That day I hadn't seen the woman from the cottage and her curtains were closed. The expensive car that was sitting in front of the cottage hadn't moved, so I was sure that they were still in there.

After we had dressed and were ready to walk out the front door, Sandy made sure that the lights were off and the beach house was secure. With all the people that would be there that day for the celebration, there was a good chance that not all of them were trustworthy.

On the boardwalk there were many people and it was still early and time for more people to arrive. The City of Santa Cruz was finishing up all of the projects that they had done and were doing. Soon it would be time for the fireworks display. We stood around and looked at the different costumes that everyone was wearing. Some people had put a bunch of work into their choice that they'd made.

Around 10:00 p.m. the festivities started. Fireworks had started exploding in the sky over the ocean. It was a beautiful site. This was something that I had dreamed about seeing for many years.

I kept looking around, waiting for Brock, and when I least expected it to happen, someone tapped me on the shoulder. After turning around, there was Prince Charming standing in front of me.

"Ellie, I knew you would come here dressed as Snow White," Brock said, smiling at me.

"You will always be my Prince Charming. You know me better than anyone," I said as I smiled back at him.

At that moment, Sandy put her hand out to shake Brock's hand. "It's nice to meet you, Brock. I am Ellie's new friend, Sandy."

"It's nice to meet you as well. I have heard nothing but good things about you from Ellie, and also about all of the fun that you two have been having," Brock replied.

Something that we weren't aware of was waiting to happen. Someone was lurking in the shadows.

"I am grateful to Ellie for coming here with me. I really needed to get away from Santa Barbara and with her being here with me, I have not only had fun, but also enjoyed peace and quiet for a week," Sandy said.

"Thank you for taking good care of her," Brock commented.

All three of us continued to stand there and watch the fireworks, and then Sandy asked us if we would like a cup of coffee. She said that she knew of a place close by that made really good coffee, and that she would like to treat us to a cup. Of course, we said that we would love some, and so she said she would be back in about half an hour.

We thanked her and she left. We weren't paying attention when she walked away, so we didn't know what direction she had taken or what coffee shop she had gone to.

It was about 11:00 p.m. and the stores were told to turn off their lights at that time, as they were going to shoot off the major fireworks. The City wanted it to be dark. The display was almost over.

When Sandy had walked into the coffee shop, there was still some light, and when she walked out with the coffee, the lighting was gone. People were holding onto each other, to make sure that no one got lost in the crowd. Brock was standing behind me with his arms wrapped around me.

We stood like that for about an hour, and then we started to worry about Sandy. Our first thought was that it was probably dark when Sandy came out of the coffee shop and maybe she had walked in the wrong direction. We stood there, looking around, trying to see her, and when the lights came back on, she was nowhere in sight.

Brock told me to walk down the boardwalk the way we had come up it, and he would go the opposite way, looking in every shop that he came to, and he wanted me to do the same. He said that we would meet back there at that spot when we found her, or even if we didn't.

What we didn't know was that Sandy had stood in line, waiting for the coffee. When she came out of the shop, a person wearing a black costume had grabbed her arm, knocking the coffee out of her hand, and stuck a gun in her back and told her that if she screamed, she and Brock and I would be dead. As they walked off the boardwalk, no one could see the gun. Everyone's eyes were on the fireworks display.

Sandy was taken to the pier and all the way there, she was told not to scream or she would get shot. She wanted to protect us and herself, so she kept quiet. When the lights came back on, no one had seen anything, and it looked like she was facing her worst nightmare.

When Brock and I met back in the same spot that we had started out at, we had no idea where Sandy could be. As we stood there, she was begging for her life. They had arrived at the place where her screams could not be heard and she was shaking and crying.

"Now that we are away from everyone, I will take off my mask and yours. That way you can see the face behind the mask."

"Why are you doing this to me?" Sandy asked with fear in her voice.

By then, the person that abducted her had taken off the mask and Sandy's as well.

"I don't know if you know who I am," said a woman.

"Yes, I do know who you are. You are Gerald's girlfriend," Sandy replied.

"I guess you do know me. What you don't know is why I am doing this. For months now, I have been trying to get Gerald to realize that he should be with me. When you kicked him out, he was staying in different motels, hiding from me, and with the excitement of the chase, this only made me want him more.

"When my husband found out about Gerald and I, he left me, calling me a two-bit whore. At the time, I stood there, laughing at him because I was convinced that I could change Gerald's mind and he would want to stay with me, and eventually love me and not you.

"After a while, the little money that I had ran out, and I had no choice but to beg my husband to come back. He refused me at first, and then I told him Gerald and I really didn't do anything that night at the convention. When Gerald ordered a drink, I put some pills in it that made him tired, and when he was stumbling around, everyone thought that he was drunk. I told him that I would help him up to his room.

"After I helped him onto the bed, he fell asleep. I took off his clothes. I did the same thing to my husband and when he went to sleep, I left the room and climbed in bed with Gerald. When he woke up, I told him that we had slept together all night, and he insisted that he wouldn't cheat on you.

"I had been watching and wanting Gerald for many months, and trying to get him in bed with me, and nothing was working until I put that pill in his drink. As Gerald was sleeping, I cuddled close to him and, even though he didn't know that I was there, lying beside him, I wanted him more than I ever did before, and was going to do anything that I needed to do to make him fall in love with me, and not you.

"The night that he came to rescue me, I had taken a couple of spark plugs out, so that my car wouldn't start. When I called him, I was sure that he would come help me. I told him that my husband was out of town. This was the perfect time for me to cause doubt in your mind about what he had done with me. I asked him to sit in the car with me the whole night, but he refused. So, while he was in there, I sprayed perfume on and made sure that the mist of it got on his jacket. I also got my lipstick out of the console and put some on. When I was putting it away, I touched the end with my finger and after I put it back, I touched his face, telling him what a gentleman he was. I also rubbed my hand across his hair. Everything was in place for him to go home to you, looking like that.

"Gerald left my car and went to sit in his car, waiting for the tow truck, not knowing that I had made arrangements for my car to be towed the next day. He sat up in his car all night, waiting for the truck to come, so he could leave and go back to you.

"When you were sitting at that light, I saw you there and again I wanted you to believe that we were having an affair. I smiled extra times at him as I wanted you to believe that we were not going to the convention, but maybe a hideaway somewhere in order to be alone at a romantic place.

"I knew that I was better for Gerald than you could ever be, and even after you kicked him out, I kept calling you, not saying anything, to keep you wondering if I was calling for Gerald and didn't want to speak to you. I wanted to keep the fighting going on between the two of you.

"I kept thinking that he would get tired of you telling him that you didn't believe him, and with this he would want to be with the woman that *did* want him.

"Everything he told you, Sandy, was true. You were too stupid to believe him.

"I left you a note on your seat in your car, telling you that I would be watching and waiting. If you found it, you probably thought that it came from Gerald. A woman that you work with, not knowing who I am, told me that you were going out of the city for a vacation and where you were going.

"I told my husband that I wanted to come here for Mardi Gras and that it would be like a second honeymoon for us. The dumb dope believed me, and I have been giving him pills ever since we got here, to keep him asleep. After enough pills, he will go to sleep forever, and then I will have his money and eventually, grief stricken Gerald, after they find your half-eaten body in the ocean days from now.

"I would have killed you before now if you hadn't brought that friend of yours, who kept watching me around the boardwalk and the amusement park. Also at your house, as I did go in to see if you were there, and you didn't even know it.

"Before I do what I came here to do to you, I will give you

a chance to ask me any questions you want to, as that will be the last thing that you will ever say," Kate said.

While Brock and I were standing on the boardwalk, wondering where to look next, I saw Gerald running up to me.

"I remember you from being at Sandy's house. Have you seen her? I am worried about her and can't find her. I think that her life could be in danger," Gerald said frantically.

"Yes, I am Ellie, and I came here to spend time with Sandy. We are worried about her as well and can't find her. Do you know where she might have gone?" I asked.

"The only other place that I can think of is the pier. I got a note from this woman that won't leave me alone, saying that she was coming here with her husband. This woman is nuts and I can't get rid of her. She has Sandy believing things that just didn't happen. I will leave her alone after we find her and I know she is safe," Gerald said.

"Let's go check out the pier. If she isn't there, we are going to need to check the beach house. She might have decided to let Ellie and me have some alone time and gone back there," Brock commented.

"I just came from there and she isn't there. If we don't find her, then we need to involve the police," Gerald said.

Brock and I followed Gerald as he started running to the pier to look for Sandy.

At the pier, Sandy continued to shake. She knew that she hadn't taken me to that place yet, and that I wouldn't even think about her being there. She wanted to keep Kate busy talking long enough for her to come up with a plan to keep herself alive.

"Yes, Kate, I do have some questions. You sure did have me fooled. I fell for everything, hook, line and sinker. Why would you want Gerald when you are already married to a man that isn't bad-looking, gives you lots of money for nice things, and does whatever you tell him to do? It makes no sense to me. You have whatever you want and your husband will buy you anything that you ask for. Apparently he loves you or he wouldn't have come back to you," Sandy said.

"You are right, Sandy. I do like money, but this way I can have both. All I am doing is keeping my husband drugged, and sooner or later his heart is going to give out," Kate replied.

"I think that Gerald is cute and all, but what is it that you love about him so much? If you let me go, I will leave here now and you can tell Gerald that you heard that I died a horrible death in a car explosion in some European country, and that there is nothing left of me. He will believe you, and I will be long gone forever. He would never find out. Then you can have him and marry him and live happily ever after. I really don't want him back, Kate. I have been trying to get rid of him for a long time now. He is more your type," Sandy commented.

"I might have some blond in my hair right now, Ellie, but I am not stupid. I know exactly what you would do. You would sing to the cops and take Gerald back. I would be in jail for many years for the crime of kidnapping you and drugging my husband, trying to kill him. You and Gerald would have the happy life. How stupid do you think that I am?" Kate said.

Sandy was standing against the railing of the pier and Kate was facing her with a gun pointed at her. Gerald and Brock were walking quietly up on Kate, and Sandy had to keep talking until they got there as she had seen them coming to help her.

"You didn't tell me what you think about Gerald that has you doing this to me, Kate," Sandy mentioned.

"Sandy, you have never seen all of Gerald's worth. He is not only gorgeous, but has the cutest smile and most beautiful eyes. Nothing personal, Sandy, but you two just aren't a match," Kate commented.

By then, Gerald was the first one standing behind Kate. He reached over her, knocking the gun out of her hand, and when he did this, Sandy moved to the side. Kate turned around and saw him looking at her with hatred in his eyes.

She accidentally fell backward over the rail on the pier and on her way down, she hit a big rock with her head before she hit the ocean water. She was floating and we had to assume she was dead.

Sandy was very happy to see Gerald. She had a lot of apologizing to do to him for not trusting or believing him. She hugged him and thanked him for saving her life. I told her that Gerald was the true hero, and he was the man who knew her the best, like no one else could.

At that time, Sandy turned to Gerald and said, "Let's go home, Gerald."

Brock and I looked at each other and smiled. That was a vacation that I would never forget. In fact, months of having Sandy in my life was nothing but an adventure of some sort. We had become the best of friends, and Brock and Gerald eventually became good friends as well.

Sometimes, when you think that you know the truth, it turns out where you don't know it all. Life is a roller coaster ride, no matter where you are. You don't need to be at an amusement park in order to enjoy it.

Our minds have a way of seeing things that our eyes don't. In the end, the truth always has a way of presenting itself.

Brock and I moved our relationship to a whole new level. We moved in together, to give it a try, just like Gerald and Sandy were doing. Once or twice a month, we would get together and come back here to Santa Cruz to either play volleyball at the beach or surf the waves. I had found a whole new enjoyment for life after I met Sandy, and I would treasure it forever.

As for Kate's husband, the police did find all kinds of drugs in his system that Kate had given him, and of course he told them that his wife was crazy! When they found Kate, they retrieved her body from the ocean. She should have known that her plan wouldn't work and she should have accepted what she did have instead of wanting something that would never be hers.

Other Books by Jana Nolan

THE OLD HENDERSON MINE

MIND POWER

SOUNDS OF FEAR

SECRETS OF SLEEPING INDIAN MOUNTAIN

PURE VENGEANCE

THE UNEXPLAINABLE

Visit her Author Web site at
JanaNolan.com

www.ingramcontent.com/pod-product-compliance
Lightning Source LLC
Chambersburg PA
CBHW061155170626
46809CB00003B/1107